ACCIDENTAL MURDERER IN APT 34

ACCIDENTAL MURDERER IN APT 34

CHISTO HEALY

Dedicated to my Uncle Jim. I miss you every day. I wish I lived in Sunnycrest where we could hang out again.

And

For Gary Smith and James Holt

If anyone deserves an apartment in the building of my success, it's the two of you.

DR. MARK STEPHENSON leaned forward in his chair, resting his arms leisurely on his desk. He smiled warmly at the man sitting across from him. The doctor's plump, round face and bald head were usually good for easing tension and making his patients feel at ease. His features were empathetic and kind. In his field, it had always done him well. However, in this particular instance his smile faded quickly, as the recipient of the gesture refused to respond.

Roger was aloof and distant. He didn't seem to notice that the doctor was in the room with him. He fidgeted nervously. His eyes danced frantically around the office like a drunken ballerina. His dusty blond mop was strewn about like he had just fought his way out of a windstorm. It was enough to put the psychiatrist's nerves on edge. He didn't need his degree to see that something was wrong.

The doctor followed his patient's gaze to the nearby window. The blinds were drawn, and the weather outside looked calm and still. Leaves fluttered from the trees, gently falling past the pane of glass. There definitely wasn't any inclement weather that would lead to his patient looking so frazzled. Maybe he was searching the sunlight for a sign of hope, some much needed strength to arm him against whatever ailed him. Dr. Stephenson frowned slightly, even though he tried his best not to do so. He worked to remain neutral no matter what he felt internally. He never wanted to discourage his patients by displaying emotions they could read into and decipher negatively.

"Roger? Can you focus on me please? I need to talk to you."

The doctor spoke in a calm and soothing tone, steady and even. His voice was as gentle and mellow as the features of his cherubic face. He had learned over time how to mask his concern and maintain composure at all times, or as today had proven, most times.

Patients were sort of like dogs. They could sense fear or worry, and they fed off it, changing their own emotions to meet the standard set for them. Once he lost control, Dr. Stephenson found it was extremely difficult to get back. It was easy to send his patient into an emotional spiral. It was a lot harder to get it back, to convince them that sad look or fearful gaze meant nothing. People listened to body language, sometimes even more than words.

Dr. Stephenson was genuinely concerned for Roger. He had only known him a short time but had already seen such a decline in the man. Roger had been skinny when he walked into this office for the first time nine months ago, but he was even thinner now, dangerously thin. The doctor couldn't help but wonder if there was an eating disorder at work here that needed to be addressed and treated.

Roger looked like he was deteriorating. Could he be sick with some kind of medical condition that he failed to mention in his paperwork? Dr. Stephenson thought maybe he should contact Roger's primary care physician and try to exchange information with her. He knew Dr. Tucci. He had shared patients with her in the past. She wanted what was best for her patients and generally worked with him to help them. Dr. Stephenson made a note on his pad that rested on the desktop to call her later. He already had Roger's signature on the necessary paperwork allowing the two of them to communicate.

Thick, dark bags rested under Roger's bloodshot eyes. Dr. Stephenson had never seen his patient in such a state before. In fact, Roger had always been one of his more pleasant sessions. His problems never seemed any worse than the average ordinary man, apart from the fact that he suffered from anxiety and depression, but even those things were fairly common diagnoses these days, as unfortunate as that was.

Dr. Stephenson and Roger had partaken in some good conversations before, but by the look of him now, today was bound to be something entirely different. Roger, himself, was different. What caused such a shift? A death in the family? He wasn't currently in a relationship as far as the doctor knew. His long-term partner had left him a long while back. He couldn't recall Roger telling him about anyone new.

"Roger? Can you talk to me? You seem distressed. We only have an hour, and I would really like to help you with whatever is bothering you."

Roger stopped his fidgeting then. His head turned to face the worried doctor. Blue eyes plagued by days of sleeplessness locked with the doctor's sympathetic gaze. Dr. Stephenson attempted to smile again, but even now that he had finally gotten his patient's attention, the gesture was still not returned. Instead, Roger shivered like a draft had just swept in behind him.

Leaning further forward, the doctor asked, "Is there something wrong, Roger? Did something happen? You look like you haven't been getting much sleep lately. Can you tell me about that?"

"I'm stressed, Doc, that's all," Roger said. The tone of his voice alone was a giveaway that his words were a serious understatement.

"Why the formalities?" Dr. Stephenson asked with another smile, trying to chip away at the ice. "You always call me Mark."

"Right. Sorry." Roger bit his lip, and lowered his eyes slightly, like a child that had done something wrong.

Mark shook his head at that reaction. "I don't want you to be sorry," he said with a small laugh. "I just want you to be comfortable. I don't know about you, but I'm a lot more comfortable with my friends than I am with my doctor. We *are* friends, aren't we, Roger?"

"Sure," Roger answered, finally forcing a smile of his own. "Though I don't usually have to pay my other friends to talk to them. That sounds like the type of friendship you might want to talk to your psychiatrist about. It may not be healthy."

The doctor clapped and laughed genuinely, relieved that the ice had finally broken. Now he just had to make sure that they didn't fall through it and drown.

"Well, I'm glad you *do* pay me," Mark Stephenson said, with a more comfortable smile. "My wife likes to eat. She doesn't talk to me for free either."

Roger smiled genuinely then. It came naturally. It was real. Mark almost sighed with relief at the sight, but he held it back.

His patient's nervousness seemed to be fading gradually. Mark had made himself a success over the years, and days like this were evidence of exactly why. He always told his patients to call him by his first name. He had found it humanized him and made things less clinical. It was easier for people to open up. Once he brought himself to their level and made things more personal and intimate, they tended to feel much more comfortable in his office.

Most people would rather confess their problems and secrets to a man, a real person, than they would to some doctor, some walking college degree that was looking down on them and judging them for their all too ordinary problems.

The formality of titles was not as important to Mark as they were to some others in his field. He had nothing to prove to the people he was trying to help. Psychiatry wasn't about power struggles. It was about diagnosis and treatment. Titles only supported egotism, which was actually detrimental to the process. It was the results that mattered the most. Negating that feeling of a doctor being in the room released a great deal of the tension normally involved in a session. Patients tended to not feel scrutinized or analyzed, like they so often did with his colleagues. He knew this for certain, because many of his colleagues' patients drifted into his care after feeling unsatisfied with their previous arrangement. On the infrequent occasion Mark Stephenson lost his patient's focus, like he had earlier with Roger, he almost always managed to get them back with the same technique and premise. Mark understood people.

Now that he had gotten Roger seemingly more comfortable, it was time for him to start really working. Sometimes, a doctor in his field needed to play detective. He needed to get information by asking the right series of questions. Mark had to look at the pieces and put the puzzle together, not even to solve the problem, but to help the patient learn how to solve it himself.

"So? Tell me what's going on, man. Is everything okay? What has you so stressed?"

Roger met his eyes again. He gave an exasperated sigh.

"It's a long story, Mark. The saying 'time is money' is quite literal when I'm in this office. I can't afford to really go into it. Besides, you'd probably have a patient waiting long before I finished telling you, someone with a shorter story, who you could offer more help to."

Mark laughed again, keeping the atmosphere lighthearted. "I'm glad your sense of humor is still intact," he said with his patented smile. "As for patients waiting, you needn't worry about that. You are my last patient of the day. Actually, you will be from now on so your long stories will only inconvenience my hungry wife." Mark chuckled and winked. "My five o'clock has left me to move onto bigger and better things."

"Maria?" Roger asked, an inquisitive look accompanying the question.

"Maria."

"I liked her," Roger said. "We talked sometimes. She seemed like a nice lady; troubled but nice."

"That's a spot-on assessment, Roger, but she didn't need my services anymore. So, that just opens things for you. If you have to go a little over, no one is going to yell at you."

"Except your wife," Roger said with a sly smile.

"No. She'll only yell at me," Mark told him. They shared a laugh.

The truth in the statement about Maria was that the woman had in fact moved on to bigger things. The better part might well have been a lie, though Mark hoped and prayed for her daily. Maria had been admitted into the Twin Spirits Psychiatric Hospital where she would be residing for quite some time. It wasn't so much that she didn't need his help anymore. It was more that she had gone beyond the capacity of his expertise. Her situation was unusual, though not necessarily unique in this city, and not what Mark Stephenson was at all trained to deal with.

He feared he was becoming more adept at handling such cases. Come to think of it, the growing number of bizarre cases were all somehow connected to the old apartment building Roger lived in: Sunnycrest Apartments. Maria lived there too, in Apartment 45, until a series of horrible tragedies destroyed her whole family. Mark didn't know if there was a real connection or if this was the work of his fanciful imagination, but one thing was for certain. Maria was more than troubled, as Roger had so tactfully put it. She was downright haunted by something. Mark shivered at the thought of it and hoped Roger didn't notice.

"Well, that's cool," Roger said, bringing Mark back from his thoughts.

Mark felt bad for drifting. He needed to focus on his current patient, not the one he already lost. *Let's not lose another,* he told himself.

Roger's eyes left the doctor and moved over to the triptych on the wall above where Mark sat. Roger's eyes traced the lines, seeming to look at how the pieces of the painting would connect if the frames were not in the way. He wasn't alone in this. Mark had selected the room's decor with very purposeful intent. Some types of art were soothing and others distracting, just as certain colors and aesthetics were comforting. There was definite strategy to this.

"I'd still have to pay for it though if I go over right?" Roger asked, his eyes still on the canvases above the doctor.

Mark smiled and leaned back comfortably in his big black leather chair.

"I'm not so worried about that," he told his patient. "I said my wife likes to eat. I didn't say she liked to eat caviar."

Roger didn't match his smile this time. He looked deep in thought about something. He chewed on his lip like it was a tough bite of steak.

"So, it's not a big deal if I go over some?" Roger lowered his gaze to meet the doctor's eyes, though his pupils seemed to tremble as if his eyes were afraid to make contact with Mark's for some reason. Mark's fingers brushed the bristles of his beard thoughtfully.

Smiling once more, Mark Stephenson shook his head. "No, it's not a big deal, my friend. I'm worried about *you*, Roger, not how long it takes for you to tell me what's wrong. So, I don't want you to worry about that either, okay? It's cool. Talk to me. Tell me what's up."

Roger nodded. He flexed his hands and rolled his neck. His leg bounced nervously.

Mark watched the man trying to relax, but whatever Roger brought with him today was clearly something that would be difficult to tell even a friend. Mark waited patiently in a relaxed posture to drive home the idea that there was no rush. Roger didn't seem to know if Mark's care and friendship was sincere or not, but that was normal. It took a great deal of trust for someone to tell their inner most secrets and feelings. Mark gave another small smile to assure that he wasn't growing impatient with the delay.

Roger voiced his concerns then. "Sometimes, I have left this office wondering if the reasons I like you are actually characteristics that make you bad at your job. It seems to me like it would be dangerous for someone in your field to care as much as you portray yourself to. If that care is genuine, then you're probably carrying a huge weight through your daily life, which probably isn't good for your wife or marriage. It almost makes me feel guilty when I tell you things. That's why I usually leave the big stuff at home, but I brought the big guns with me today. I'd be lying if I said I wasn't hesitant to burden you with such things, but I am definitely in a place where I need help and can't do it on my own. Unless, of course, your care isn't real and it's all an act, in which case, you need therapy just as badly as I do because you would have to be a sociopath or a psychopath or something. The idea of that doesn't make me want to open up either. It's kind of a rock and a hard place type of situation, you know?"

Roger punctuated the speech with a long drawn out sigh.

Mark looked taken aback. This was one instance where he felt it was actually important to let his emotions show. Roger needed him to be authentic. He blinked.

"Wow," he said. "There's a lot to unpack there." The doctor took a deep breath and sat up straight. He nodded. "First off, you're not wrong. Most therapists and psychologists as well as psychiatrists like myself end up needing mental health help just like you do. I believe that is *because* we're good at our jobs, not the other way around. Rest assured, I am neither a sociopath nor a psychopath. If need be, I can show you the paperwork to prove it." He gave a beaming smile and drew one from his patient as well. "I assure you, buddy. My care and concern is definitely genuine."

"Okay. I'll tell you," Roger said with a slow, deep breath to steady his nerves, his leg still tapping nervously. "Alice is back." When the words left his lips, his quivering eyes immediately fell away from the doctor's gaze and rested on his lap. His hands worked nervously at his hair. Mark's eyebrows raised with interest.

"Alice? I'm sorry if I have forgotten something you've told

me in past sessions, Roger, but I can't seem to recall who Alice is. Can you please remind me?"

Roger glanced up quickly, but immediately looked right back down. He was staring at his upturned palms as if they were coated in blood.

"Nah," he said quietly, "I never told you about her. I don't talk about her to anyone. Ever."

Mark leaned further forward, his curiosity causing his brow to furrow. "I'm sorry, Roger. I didn't hear the last thing you said. Maybe my age is catching up to me. It might be time to get a hearing aid, but then I can't pretend I don't know my wife is yelling at me. Would you please repeat what you just said?"

Roger looked up at him, his eyes watery and unsteady. He was frowning. He looked almost as if he were in mourning. His expression bore the same emotion as the grieving widow Mark had spoken to earlier in the day. It took Mark away briefly, to a day that was lodged in his mind. He pictured himself standing under a black umbrella being pelted by relentlessly falling rain at the back of a funeral he never wanted to go to but was forced to for his own mental health. Mark put the vision out of his head quickly, and reminded himself to deal with his own problems on his own time. This was Roger's time.

"I said no," Roger told him. His voice was louder, and he was speaking more clearly, but the word seemed to quiver slightly with the anticipation of fresh tears. He cleared his throat in an attempt to regain composure. "I never told you about her."

"That's good," the doctor said with a sigh of relief followed by yet another smile. "I was beginning to think my age really was catching up to me. I thought it could be senility. Glad to know I'm safe from that for now. Would you like to tell me about her today, to explain who Alice is? I would like to know. It would help me to understand what you're dealing with."

"Not really," Roger said with a frown deep enough to counter the doctor's smile completely. It was truly the anti-smile. "It feels like talking about it gives it power, like I'm unlocking a box and letting something evil into the world. God, that sounds crazy even to me."

Mark raised his eyebrows. "It doesn't sound crazy to me, Roger. Though I will admit it has me curious. Fill me in. Please? You're here, and there's obviously something about this Alice that's troubling you. I'm stuck in a bad position, unable to help you if I don't understand what's going on. Can you tell me about Alice?"

Roger broke into awkward, nervous laughter. "*Alice* is troubling me. You don't know the half of it, Mark."

"No, I don't. I can't, not if you won't tell me."

Roger's frown deepened even more than the doctor would have thought possible. It looked like there was a magnet pulling his face toward the floor of the office, like any more force would tear it right from his skull.

"Okay, fine. I'll tell you," Roger relented. "I'm sure this defies doctor patient privilege, but I've been feeling guilty for so long, I suppose it doesn't matter anymore. I'm exhausted, Mark. If you rat me out, I don't even care. I won't blame you or hold it against you. My payment for Alice is overdue anyway. Maybe it would even relieve some of my guilt if I was finally held responsible."

Mark kept it from being visible, but he felt a little nervous. Sometimes, people beat themselves up for things and treated their sins like crimes, but anytime a patient mentioned being ratted out, it suggested something illegal. If that actually was the case, depending on the severity, Mark could actually have information that would aid a criminal investigation and things would get complicated fast since he was forbidden to release that information. He hoped that wasn't the case. He didn't like to involve the police, and, even more, he didn't like to be in a position where he felt morally obligated to but unable to due to the restraints of the law. Mark went through this with Maria already recently. It was a tough spot to be in, to put it mildly. Under the desk, Mark crossed the fingers of his right hand.

"Responsible for what, Roger? I don't understand. You don't

have to worry about me ratting you out for anything you did in your past. I'm actually forbidden to do so. I'm bound by doctor patient privilege. This is a safe place, Roger, the place where you can open up about the things that aren't safe to tell other people. Okay? But your vagueness and ambiguity is confusing. You're losing me here, Roger. I need you to clarify and explain clearly."

"Alice is dead."

THE WORDS FELL in the quiet room like hand grenades.

The doctor's eyebrows rose as his eyes threatened to pop out of his skull and roll across his desktop to drop onto the floor and rest at Roger's feet. So much for containing emotions. At least Roger would know he was being authentic. Mark closed his eyes for a second to regain composure and then reopened them.

"I'm sorry. You caught me off guard with that one. How did she die? What happened to Alice? No. Wait. Scratch that. I'm sorry. We're getting ahead of ourselves here. Let's go back to the beginning. Start by telling me who she is. Who is Alice?"

"Was," Roger said solemnly, looking away. "Who she *was*."

"My apologies. You're right. I'm sorry. Who was she?"

Roger nodded. "I've been living over at the Sunnycrest Apartments for two years now."

Now it was the doctor's turn to nod. He got more patients from that apartment building than he cared to admit. There was something wrong with that place, something dark. Maria was proof of that.

"Yes. I've seen it in your paperwork," he said. "Apartment 34."

"Right, well...when I first moved in, there was a girl who lived across the hall in Apartment 33. Her name was Alice."

Roger had followed his sister Kara to the city. Kara had always been a force to be reckoned with, someone who knew what she wanted and went after it. She took charge of life. Roger had always been jealous of her ability to do that. She was his big sister and he looked up to her. Kara was like a superhero to her shy, introverted sibling. With Roger's social anxiety, he feared he wouldn't make it through life without her. So, the big city it was. The large, noisy, terrifying place was still safer than home without Kara.

The city opened doors for Roger, doors he didn't know existed back home. He met a girl, Lisa, at a comic book convention, something he had never been able to attend before moving here. She was gorgeous with dark brown hair and bright green eyes, way out of Roger's league in his opinion. Despite their contrasting personalities, as Lisa was far more extroverted, more like Kara, she seemed to really like Roger. She enjoyed science fiction and horror as much as he did. It was Lisa that set things in motion. It wasn't intentional, just fate, Roger supposed.

Kara helped Roger find an apartment. Sunnycrest was old and a little bit creepy, but it was a fine, sturdy building. It had character and seemed like it should be a historical landmark or something. The building was full of interesting people, and many of them socialized with each other, though only a few took the time to converse with Roger, and sadly he was glad for that. If they did start a conversation with him, he tended to awkwardly stumble through it, and they tended not to start a second one. Then he felt embarrassed each time he saw them. Roger chose to avoid those terrible feelings by avoiding the conversations altogether. He offered a smile or a wave when they were in the hallway at the same time, but then he would fumble with his keys and hurry into his apartment. His neighbors probably thought he was nuts.

Mostly, it was the staff who continued to speak to him: the groundskeeper, the janitor, and the old woman who came around to collect the rent money. The rest mostly gazed at him with a look he read as, *is he on drugs?*

Deep down, Roger wished he was better able to be a part of the world. He wished he could make friends with his neighbors and trade quips with them on their way in or out. It just wasn't in his skill set. His failed attempts at it only made him feel worse. It was a minor miracle that he didn't chase Lisa off. At least by that point, he hadn't.

Unable to speak to people, Roger tended to watch them instead. He noticed there was no mother with the family of his new neighbors across the hall. It was just a young girl, maybe six or seven years old, and her dad. The dad looked tired, and Roger imagined he would be, working full time and being a single parent. Those weren't shoes Roger would want to step in if he had a choice. Children were even harder to understand than adults.

Roger didn't know where the mother was. If she had lived there, she had left or passed away before Roger moved into Apartment 34. She never even seemed to visit her daughter, which struck Roger as strange. Such behavior was more common for fathers than for mothers from what Roger had seen throughout life. He hadn't heard much talk about dead beat moms. Yet, Alice's mother never showed in the time they shared the hall at Sunnycrest Apartments. Roger couldn't help but wonder if she would have, had that time not been cut short.

Roger didn't interact much with the girl's dad. His name was Brian and Roger only knew that much from reading the label on the mailbox. Brian had a mean look about him. Sometimes Roger would try a smile or a wave, which took great effort for him, and the man would just stare back at him with intense brown eyes circled by the dark rings of sleeplessness, his mouth drawn in a tight line. It made Roger feel wholly uncomfortable.

One day, the first day that Roger could tie the story back to, Lisa had come over for a date night. She showed up with a glowing smile, a brand-new bag of hot fries, and a blue ray of an eighties movie they both adored and longed to watch the bonus features of. It had the makings of a good night, but that quickly changed.

Brian was in the hallway screaming. They could hear him through the thick, old apartment door, his footfalls like the bangs of a bass drum adding a backbeat to his bellowing anger.

Lisa cringed and winced at the sharp sounds of his yells like they were actual physical objects hurled at her face. She would hug herself and look to Roger for help. Roger's own nerves had him trembling, but he frowned at her discomfort and tried to hug her, to help her feel safe. He raised the volume on the television, but it was a futile effort.

Finally, she pulled away and looked at him with a blend of fear and disgust. "How can you just sit around and listen to that?" she asked sharply.

Why can't you be more of a man? Roger silently added for her. Out loud, he simply sighed before gazing at the door between him and the screaming man in the hall. He swallowed the lump that rose in his throat. He could still feel Lisa staring at him and he didn't know what to do.

Roger didn't have the heart to tell her it happened all the time, that he was skilled at tuning other people out, that the idea of confronting such a man was far more disturbing to him than listening to him yell in the hallway. Brian was frightening when he wasn't yelling. He had an intimidating presence, and Roger didn't need anyone to tell him that he wasn't.

When Lisa wasn't around and Brian would commit a hostile takeover of the hall, Roger would turn the television up as loud as it took or turn the stereo on. He knew what Lisa would think of him if he behaved that way now. It was written all over her face.

Roger would have left, taken Lisa elsewhere to try and salvage the night, but he couldn't do so without walking past the angry man. He thought about calling the police, even if just to make a noise complaint, but he knew Alice and her dad had lived there long before he moved in. No one else on the seventh floor seemed to have called on him before. He would reel it in if they had, right?

Roger feared Brian would know it was him who called. Behind his eyes, he pictured the man's angrily stoic stare. If he knew that Roger tried to get him in trouble, then his anger would be directed at Roger, and Roger doubted Lisa was going to step in and protect him. Bravery was not one of the ingredients God had thrown into the mix during his creation. Roger knew since Tommy Warbucks had slapped him silly on the playground in sixth grade that fighting wasn't in his wheelhouse, and Brian made Tommy look like a field mouse.

Roger didn't know what to tell Lisa, what to say to comfort her or repair her damaged opinion of him. It made him withdraw and give in to his anxiety. He shrugged his shoulders without a word, and that seemed to upset her even more.

Roger was at a loss. It felt unfair. He wished she had more empathy for his own issues. Still, he didn't want to lose her. She was one of the best parts of his life, a dream made real. He reached for her hand, but she tugged it away, and when she did, she might as well have slapped him. Roger didn't know how to make her understand that this was just part of his life, something he was forced to accept and live with, unless he found somewhere else to live and moved out of Sunnycrest, but he was tied to a lease for the next year at least.

Alice shrieked, full on wailing, hysterical sobs, adding to the chaos in the hall, and it was more than Lisa could take. That child screamed in agony that matched her father's anger, a chorus of harmonizing tragedy. Roger was forced to listen to this day in and day out, but Lisa wasn't going to. It was nerve racking and scary to her. Her face was flushed, and her eyes were wet. Roger tried to make up for his lack of words with physical affection. He put his arms around her.

Lisa threw her own fit of anger then, shoving him off her and onto his back on the couch when he lost his footing. She threw the Blu-ray case at him and stormed out of the apartment only to loudly slam the door behind her, which made Roger jump as if she had physically struck him. He waited without breathing to listen and see if she got involved in the conflict out there. He felt an overwhelming, terrible fear she would, and Brian would turn on her. Then Roger would have no choice but to act, despite knowing it wouldn't end well.

However, she didn't say anything more to Brian than she said to Roger. She just stormed by, the click clack of her heels standing apart from the pounding of Brian's work boots. Roger sighed with relief, though it was followed by a wave of shame. He was going to have do something to remedy the situation, or he was going to lose Lisa for good and he knew it. He didn't know if he had the ability to fix it, if he had what it took. He couldn't talk to his neighbors. How could he manage a serious relationship? How could he find a new apartment, break his lease, confront Brian, or do any of the things that would make her feel better?

Roger just slumped back on his couch and cried, but his own tears were much quieter than Alice's.

The next day, he sent Lisa roses and a first edition Nightbreed comic book in hopes of smoothing things over. He knew that even if it worked, it would be temporary, a band-aid on a bad situation. He needed to solve the actual problem, and the more he thought about it, the more anxiety attacks he had. He found himself at the liquor store buying a bottle of harsh whiskey to help settle his nerves. He would sip it and feel the heat flow through his core, and it would relax him, remind him how to breathe.

Roger didn't think this was something he could answer on his own, so he paid a visit to his big sister, the person he'd turned to for advice his entire life up to this point. Kara was on her way out when he got there. It seemed to Roger that Kara was always on her way out. She was just that type of person, built for city life, always on the go.

"Come with me if you want to talk. Walk fast," she said.

Roger frowned but he did his best to keep up. It was hard to gather his thoughts while rushing down the street, but he stumbled through the situation with Alice and her dad and the rift it had caused with Lisa. When they got to the subway station, Roger felt like he was practically chasing her down the flights of stairs.

"So, what do you think?" he called from behind her.

Kara turned and patted his shoulder before passing through the turnstiles. "I think Lisa's right, little brother. You don't have to confront the dude yourself, but you should at least call somebody. You've always been one to do the right thing, Rodge. That's part of your charm. Don't ruin it now."

Before he could reply, the train pulled up and Kara pushed her way through people to get on it.

Roger sighed but made his way back up the steps, much slower this time, his mind on all the possible terrible things that could come of following his sister's advice. He felt bad about what she said though and his heart sank as he emerged from the darkness of the subway into the light of day. He had always been someone who tried to do right, until the anxiety started. It was hard to do right when your mind cycled through all the possibilities of what could go wrong. He still wanted to be a good person. He did. He was just afraid. Always. He was always afraid. It was horrible.

When Roger got back home, he looked at the cracked brick and the shadows cast by the trees, and he couldn't help but think the building looked a bit creepy. It hadn't felt bad to him before. Maybe it was just another stab of his relentless anxiety. He began to think wild thoughts as he entered, imagining the building was alive. What if Alice's dad was possessed, and what if the lease had actually been some kind of contract for his soul? He knew these thoughts were not even close to rational, but he couldn't keep them at bay. That was how anxiety worked. He looked at the neighbors he passed on his way up to his apartment, trying to force a smile for each of them. None of them seemed to be afraid of Sunnycrest. Most of them seemed downright normal, waving and offering him greetings if they weren't involved in a phone call.

Roger felt like he was being ridiculous. He hated having anxiety and wondered why he did. If it was genetic, his sister certainly didn't get it. He blamed his father for it. Roger blamed his father for everything. When the rickety elevator stopped and he reached his floor, the doors creaked and moaned their way open, and Brian's furious face stared at him.

Roger's eyes went wide. He thought the man was angry at him, but then Alice's dad ran off down the hall, screaming her name. Roger's shoulders slumped and he sighed with relief, but his heart wasn't willing to slow back down just yet. He looked both ways repeatedly as he made his way to his apartment door, checking for the wild man. He was nervous and afraid, fidgeting enough to drop his keys, which made his heart pound even harder in his thin chest.

When he bent down to retrieve them, Brian's screams of rage rang out behind him, and Roger jumped, banging his head on the door. He winced in pain and closed one eye against the immediate headache. With trembling hands, he grabbed his keys, the man still bellowing his anger at his young daughter behind him. Alice shrieked and sobbed, adding to the cacophony of madness.

Roger had had his fill. He opened his door and slid into his apartment, quickly closing and locking it with shaking hands. Then he leaned his back against it and slid to the floor. Why did he have to be such a coward, so afraid of everything? He felt so weak and incompetent, unworthy of a woman like Lisa.

After that, Roger had trouble sleeping. He would toss and turn and have nightmares about Brian's face contorting and stretching as he bellowed his anger, grabbing Alice with claw-like, demonic hands and ripping her apart before turning his elongated face toward Roger as the horns burst from his scalp. Roger would squeeze his eyes shut so tightly it hurt, clap his hands over his ears, and wait for death, because he was frozen immobile, and it was all he could do.

He would wake up in a cold sweat, his heart full of guilt at his own inaction in both his dream life and the waking world. Roger just wanted a normal life. That's all he wanted. Why was something so simple so hard to achieve? His guilty heart left him wondering if Alice was across the hall wondering the very same thing.

"I couldn't take it, Mark," Roger said to the doctor as he bit down on his trembling lip, tears welling in his eyes.

"Understandably. No decent man would have an easy time with such a thing, Roger, especially someone with anxiety. That sounds really difficult. I don't think I would have had an easy time with something like that myself. And you didn't ask for any of that. All you did was find a place to live. You'd be surprised to discover how many of my patients are people with problem neighbors. It's unfortunately common, and it really sucks."

"Maybe that's true, Mark, but this goes far beyond that, and I am not a decent man. There was a time when I might have been, but that time is long since gone."

"I don't think that's true," Mark countered. "You've always seemed like a decent fellow to me. I've known men who contained no decency, more than I've cared to. You're definitely not one of then, Roger."

"It *is* true." Roger exhaled. "You haven't seen my true colors. When I finish the story, your opinion of me will change. You'll see. There's a lot more to tell."

The doctor failed to hide his emotions again. He frowned deeply and sat back to listen to the rest of the story.

Roger eyed him for a moment, then reluctantly continued, "One day, I was down the hall at the laundry room."

Roger hadn't brought his clothes with him over to the laundry room. He liked to get things set up first. It was a small room with a single washer and dryer and a box on the wall that dispensed powdered soap and fabric softer in exchange for quarters. Roger worried that if he forgot his change and had already filled the washer with his clothes that someone else would be inconvenienced. Then they would think badly of him, and he feared that negative view would spread to other neighbors and his whole building would hate him. So, he developed a plan to avoid that outcome. He'd prepare his clothes in a garbage bag and keep them by his apartment door. Then he would go purchase the soap and start the machine with nothing in it and return to retrieve his clothes. This day was no different.

At least not at first.

Roger tried to put his quarter in the slot in the box on the wall. He was ever so slightly off with his trajectory and the coin bounced off the box and onto the floor. Roger grumbled curse words under his breath as he got to his hands and knees to find where it had finally stopped after careening around the floor on its edge like a silver wheel. This was exactly why he didn't bring the clothes right away.

A scream rang out. It wasn't Brian. It was Alice. She just let loose this high-pitched, ear-piercing shriek of defiance. Roger, on all fours, looked up at the door. He heard the stamping of her small feet running by. The sound was followed by her father's anger. Brian demanded she return to him at once. Roger was just staring at the door, the quarter long forgotten, wondering what to do.

The screaming was just on the other side of the door. He felt trapped. He couldn't make it back to his apartment without crossing that river of anger that flowed between. Roger did his best to silently get to his feet, moving impossibly slow, his eyes trained on the laundry room door, waiting for Alice's father to come bursting through, foaming at the mouth.

The violence sounded like it had gone back to their own apartment, at least for the moment. Roger was too busy holding his breath to even sigh with relief. He crept toward the laundry room door, still trembling and afraid, but listening.

Roger could hear the crying getting louder, more hysterical. The child was throwing a serious fit. Roger shook his head. He froze with his hand on the door and wished he could tell her not to, tell her that her fit would bring a far worse fit from her father. His mind showed him various tragedies that could come from such a thing: her father beating her with household items until she lay dead on the floor; her father growing angrier by the moment as he searched for her, kicking the laundry room door open and venting that anger upon Roger; her father pulling a gun and shooting at her, killing her and Roger in the process with a stray bullet. He imagined Alice running and looking back at her wild father and losing her step in the process, tumbling over the railing in the stairwell and landing broken at the bottom.

Then Roger heard the smashing of wood and the shattering of glass. He realized with all too clear terror that it wasn't conjured by his imagination. The new sounds were very real and very close. He took a deep breath or tried to, but his breath was caught in his chest and wouldn't come willingly. He should have just fled the room, run for his apartment, and hid there until it was over, like he had done so many times before.

Roger tried to think about what his sister had told him, that he was someone who always did the right thing. He wanted to still be that person, anxiety be damned. He thought about Alice. If it was this frightening to him, how terrifying must it be to be a child like her? It had to be so awful. It was an unfair, terrible life that she didn't have the power to change on her own. She needed help, someone to stand up for her, to get her out, to make her father stop. It wasn't a role Roger wanted to volunteer for, but it seemed like he was the only person around and he knew the truth in his heart already; he had left this child to her own devices for far too long as it was. He couldn't do it any longer.

It was madness, but Roger stepped out into the hall and stared at their door, Apartment 33. He had done this many times before, when the anger was contained within and hadn't bled out into the hallway. He hadn't the faintest idea why when he knew damn well, he was way too much of a coward to do anything about what was going on within those walls.

On one such occasion, Roger knocked. He was trembling and terrified, but he told himself enough was enough and he was going to finally say something to Brian about his behavior. When the door opened and Roger found himself looking the man in his powerful eyes, Roger turned away and ran down the hall. He bypassed the elevator, not wanting to wait for it to come, and pounded his way down the stairs and out the building where he stared back at the entrance waiting for Brian to emerge with a vengeance. He cursed himself as he worked to catch his breath. Sometimes, he wished he was someone else, someone stronger and more capable, but he wasn't. He was Roger, and that was all he was ever going to be.

To make matters worse, he feared for Alice. His anxiety had already showed him countless possible scenarios to explain the tragic repercussions of a visit from a disturbed neighbor. The man would surely blame the child for drawing Roger to their house and embarrassing him. She would get screamed out, punished, and beaten worse than she already did, and that would be on him. The idea that something terrible would happen to that child and it would be his fault was not something Roger could live with.

Was it really any different what he was already doing? Wasn't he still guilty for turning a blind eye to her suffering? Wasn't he just as much at fault for allowing it to happen and doing nothing to intervene? As much as he didn't like it, he told himself that the answer was yes.

As he stood in that hall staring at the partially open door to Apartment 33, he told himself today had to be different. Today, *he* had to be different. He had to be the man that Kara and Lisa thought him to be and do something to stop this and help that poor child. As if on cue, her cries rose to a crescendo. Brian peered through the open door at Roger, his eyes so open they seemed swollen. Then a big hand of thick calloused fingers came to slam the door closed.

Roger's body matched the jump of his startled heart, but he remained there, frozen to the old tiles just as he had been in his nightmares. He was panting heavily, on the verge of hyperventilation, and willing himself not to cut and run again. He was so scared, but he was always scared. That was life with crippling anxiety, a life that no one seemed to understand. Roger had to face fear every day and he had to overcome it in order to live. He was more capable than he gave himself credit for. Roger took a big inhale and let it out slowly to ease his racing heart. Something slammed against the other side of the door and Roger jumped, squeezing his eyes shut tight and clenching his hands into fists.

What if that was Alice? It could have been her head banging against the door. *You can't run,* he told himself. *Not this time. You can't. Come on, Roger. Man up.*

Something banged against the door again.

3

MARK STEPHENSON SHOOK HIS HEAD. He forgot all about the clock. His mind was on the story. The way Roger told it, Mark could see it in his mind, almost see himself in the role, and feel what it had been like for an introvert like Roger to go through something like that. Sometimes being an empath made being a psychiatrist easier, and other times it made it heavier and harder to carry.

He wasn't sure what stopped Roger, what paused the movie in his mind, as his eyes seemed to still focus on the screen. "Roger, do you need a minute?"

"What? Oh, no. I'm okay. Sorry."

Mark nodded. "Please, go on. I want to know the rest, to know what happened that day."

Roger frowned, but he nodded. With his right hand, Mark massaged some of the growing tension from his face.

Roger stared at him with an intensity that made the doctor feel uneasy before he continued, "As I was standing there, the door opened."

Alice burst out of the door right in front of Roger, the filthy old doll she never let go of dangling from her small hand. He could do nothing. He was frozen in place, his feet cemented to the tiles of the hallway. The small girl was hysterical. There was a cut on the side of her face, fresh and bleeding down her chin. She looked up at Roger with wild eyes, an animalistic quality to them. She started running right toward her frozen neighbor, her eyes wide with terror.

Roger came to life as if a spell had been broken. The fear in the child's face gave life to his limbs. Suddenly he found himself able to move, to react. An angel on his shoulder was propelling him forward, commanding him to save her. It was time. He had to move, to act, to put an end to her torment. He had to be the man Kara saw him as, the man Lisa wanted him to be. He surged forward.

Roger, the man who lived guided by fear, transformed into a completely different state, something unbeknownst to him. It was a primal instinct, a gut reaction, like he wasn't behind the wheel of his own vehicle. He grabbed Alice and scooped her up into his arms, and then he quickly ducked back into the laundry room. "Shhh, be quiet," he said into the child's ear. "I've got you. It's okay. You're safe now."

Roger did his best to shut the door without making a sound. The slight clicking of it falling into place made his skin crawl with beetles of nerves, the power of anxiety returning. He listened intently for the trembling child's furious father, the booming sound of his angry steps echoing through the acoustics of the ancient hallway.

Roger didn't know what to do next. He didn't think ahead. He just reacted. If the man came through that door, would Roger try to defend the child? Would he fight for her? Did his courage extend that far? He wished he had the answers to those questions.

Roger was aware that the chances of getting caught were high. The door to the laundry room had no windows. It was solid metal covered in chipped green paint, with rust showing from beneath. He could listen for the angry yells, for the footsteps, but he couldn't know for sure when the coast would be clear. He knew he couldn't stay in this tiny room forever. Eventually, he'd have to make a break for it and attempt to get the girl to the elevator or the stairs, but his heart thundered. His mind played for him all the different ways it could go wrong. He wished desperately that he had a way to turn it off. It wasn't making this any easier.

Roger tried to keep his focus on the sounds of the larger man's footsteps and keep his mind off the yells directed at Alice, the demands that she return immediately or suffer terrible consequences. The screams were deceiving. They bounced off the walls and sounded like they came from anywhere and every-where. The footsteps were the real clues, the sounds of what direction he was going, how close or how far he truly was.

Roger hoped to hear the sound of the stairwell door or the elevator's chime. That would be his green light telling him to go. He couldn't wait forever though. If that sound didn't come, he was going to have to wait for the footsteps to be far away, at the other end of the long hall. Then he could tear the door open and run.

He decided he couldn't wait for the elevator. It would give Alice's father too much time to catch up, take his daughter back, and make Roger pay for his interference. The same dangers lurked if Roger were to take her back to his own apartment. Because of Roger's anxiety, he locked the door every time he left, even just to go to the laundry room. It was too risky to try to retrieve his keys and unlock the door with the girl in his arms before her father got to them. The stairwell was the safest bet, the choice with the least amount of possible bad outcomes. Maybe anxiety was useful after all.

Even with the decision made on where to go and what to do, Roger still trembled as much as the girl in his arms. He was as frightened as he'd ever been.. Even minimizing the chances of what could go wrong, the wrong that remained was more than Roger's anxiety-ridden mind was willing to contemplate.

He could be beaten or killed at Brian's hands. He saw the level of the man's anger, knew how boundless it was. What would stop Brian once he got started, once his fists were working on Roger's skull? If Roger did get Alice out of the building, what would stop her father from reporting her missing? Maybe he would have seen who took her and say she was kidnapped. How would Roger explain the truth to the authorities? Would they ever believe him? Would Alice corroborate what he was saying? He knew enough to know that someone like him wouldn't make it in prison.

Roger said a silent prayer to a God he wasn't sure he even believed in, begging to be guided out safely and to get the child the help she needed. Deep down in his quivering bones, he hoped that someone was listening.

Mark had his fingers on his lips. He didn't know what to say. It wasn't often that he was at a loss for words. His job required him to find the words when his patients couldn't. He struggled to remember his role, to shake off the feelings conjured by the story. He swore the air changed in the room.

Swallowing a rising lump in his throat, he finally said, "I- I'm sorry, Roger. That sounds terribly frightening. I can see that day was a source of great trauma for you."

"You haven't heard the worst of it yet."

Those words made Mark nervous once more. He tried not to show it, but his breath caught in his chest. He forced a smile and fiddled with a paperclip under the desk, out of sight from Roger's eyes. "Okay," he said with a nod. "Go on then. Tell me."

Roger answered with a nod of his own. Mark watched as his eyes left the here and now and returned to the land of his memories, with his horror and trauma. Mark knew it wasn't professional, but he wanted to go around the desk and put a supportive hand on the man's shoulder, hug him even. He just squeezed the paperclip in his hand, point pressing into his palm.

Roger began again, "I heard her father in the hallway. He was furious, mad with rage, like a monster from a fairy tale."

Roger was terrified, possibly more frightened than the child he was trying to save. He became painfully aware that he wasn't cut out to be a hero. He felt pathetic, emasculated by his own fear.

Just then, Alice started wheezing. She was coughing hard, a loud, dry, terrible cough. Roger feared the consequences of such loud sounds. He thought she'd just gotten herself worked up from the stress of the situation and the cough was accompanying her cry. The tears had never stopped, a product of fear and screaming. Roger knew if her father heard her coughing, they were both going to be in big trouble.

"Come on. It's okay," he whispered into her ear. "I'm going to get you out of here, get you somewhere where you will be safe, okay? But you have to be quiet, honey. You have to try to stop coughing. Please, Alice. If he catches us, he will kill us. Just quiet down now. Focus on your doll, okay. Let her comfort you. You can do this."

Alice didn't answer. She was perspiring, her skin cool and clammy. When he looked down at her, he saw she'd gone pale. She must have been so afraid. He knew how frightened he was, but he couldn't imagine what it was like to be in her tiny black shoes, to live with that fear every day, to have to answer to it. Well, he could understand it to some degree that now that he thought about it. That was exactly what anxiety was like.

Still, he felt for the child. He wanted even more to save her from that life. If someone could have saved him from his monster that clung to him every day, he would have begged them for it. He wanted to do for her what he couldn't do for himself. He wanted desperately to free her, and he knew all too well that he would never get the chance if she didn't quiet down, if she didn't cease that horrible, dry coughing.

"Please," he whispered again with his hand over her mouth.

Mark covered his mouth with the palm of his hand. His own stare grew intense as he thought about that poor child and this poor man. Maybe Roger's assessment of Mark wasn't off base, and he did feel things too much. Maybe he wasn't so good at his job after all. The empath in him was taking the reins. Something about this story, about the truth of it, the raw emotion, the guilt and remorse that was emanating from the storyteller, hit him hard, right in the core of his being. He felt like crying. He wouldn't. He would never allow that to happen when he was with a patient, but he felt it. He felt it like the grip of a giant fist wrapped around him.

Mark saw Roger notice the man across from him growing uncomfortable and he frowned, hoping it didn't cause him to stop the story. He didn't want Roger to shut down.. They had already gone too far for that. There was no turning back now. Maybe it was selfish but Mark needed to know the rest.. He could also see that Roger had been holding all of this for some time. He needed to finally be unburdened, to put his truth out

into the world, and this was the safest place for him to do that..
Roger took a breath. Unconsciously, Mark echoed the gesture.
He rubbed at his face as Roger wiped the sweat from his palms
onto his pants legs and licked at his lips. Then he resumed his
tale.

"I covered her mouth with my hand."

Alice was being loud, not louder than the bellowing monster
in the hall, but loud enough to be heard should that beast stop
for a breath. Roger was afraid they would be heard and discovered, that his good deed would come to a terrible conclusion. If
Alice's father were to kill them both, Roger would have failed
the child and paid for it with his own life. It would have all been
for nothing. Roger couldn't allow that to happen.

He had asked her to be quiet, done his best to calm her, but
he hadn't gotten through. Maybe she was so used to running,
screaming, and crying, she wasn't able to see there could be
another option. Roger's heart ached for her. He understood
how easy it was to believe that your terrible routine was the
only reality, but he was determined to show her a different path,
to prove to her that it could get better, and to prove it to
himself.

Alice's father screamed her name, roared it, the syllables
drawn out like a hell song. The furious sound was accompanied
by stomping up and down the hallway like a mad bull charging
back and forth past the laundry room. Alice's trembling had
turned into full on spasming gyrations. Roger's eyes floated
between her and the door. Alice seemed to be having some kind
of fit, a seizure or something like it. The door was the only thing
between them and certain death. Suddenly, Roger felt over-

whelmed by terror. Something was wrong with Alice and who was he going to ask for help? Her father?

Opening that door would get them both killed but staying there when he had no idea what to do wasn't going to do them any good either. He was in a horrible state of panic, his own breathing coming in quick bursts. Tears ran lines down his face leaving streaks like cheap window cleaner on a mirror.

Roger let go of Alice and laid her on the floor before him, cringing at how cold the ground was. For the first time, he wished he had brought his clothes with him. He would have had something to lay beneath her, something warm to wrap her in. With eyes on the door that stood between them and the roaring beast in the hall, Roger struggled to ease his phone from his pocket. He was shaking something awful now, but it was nothing compared to whatever was happening to poor Alice. Her muscles seemed to tense and relax and tense again, forcing her into terrible positions.

"Help me. What do I do?" he whispered to her. "How do I help?"

The child said nothing. She just coughed and wheezed and grasped at the air between them with her fingers bent in a claw-like position, her other hand gripping the filthy half naked doll she carried everywhere. Roger's stream of tears picked up its pace, a wild river now, pouring like rain down his cheeks. He pressed the volume button on his phone until it was in the red and he knew it wouldn't give their position away. Then he called Kara. If anyone would know what to do, it would be his sister.

"You've reached Kara. I'm busy as usual, doing what I do. Leave a message and I will get back to you as soon as life allows it. Sorry for the inconvenience. Love you." His sister's voice was followed by a singular beep telling him it was time to leave a message.

Roger's left hand balled into a tight fist. His right hand squeezed the phone until his knuckles went bone white. He tried to call Lisa and had much the same result. He grit his teeth, fighting back the scream in his throat. He wanted to throw his phone. He had wanted to help, to save this child. Now something terrible was happening and he was caught there not knowing what to do or how to fix it. Would she have wound up in this state if he had done nothing? Would she have hyperventilated and seized with or without him? Had he exacerbated it by putting his hand over her mouth. Was it his fault? Did he do this to her? There were so many questions, so many terrible questions, but no answers to be found outside of what was in his heart: he was responsible.

Roger heard the feet stop outside the laundry room. He felt himself stop breathing. He heard Brian's voice call for his daughter, speak her name in a voice hoarse from screaming. "Alice?"

Roger was afraid that it was all over. He grabbed the child off the floor, cringing as he dropped his phone and it clattered to the ground. He was trying so hard to be quiet. There were no footsteps for a moment. No sound at all, aside from Roger's heartbeat booming in his ears.

He was backed up against the wall, watching the door in horror, just waiting to be discovered and broken by the violent hands of her father. He held Alice close to him and whispered into her ear, his voice quivering with the fear in his heart, that everything was going to be alright, though something in his gut told him that was far from the truth. The anxiety that always stayed with him screamed to him now as well, telling him that everything had gone to hell and he was a filthy liar, attempting to give false hope to a sick and frightened child.

Roger didn't even realize at first that Alice was no longer moving, that she rested as still and lifeless in his arms as the plastic doll that rolled from her now open hand onto the tile floor. When he did, his heart sank. He suppressed a scream, and stared, wide-eyed in terror at her still form, finally taking his eyes off the door despite the fact the footsteps hadn't moved away. He no longer cared what happened to him. He had failed her, failed her in the worst way possible.

Roger didn't know exactly when Alice had died. She could have been dead in his arms for several minutes, with his foolish bravado convincing him to whisper into her unhearing ear that it was going to be okay. It was anything but okay. This was the worst thing that could have happened. Even if he somehow made it out of this tiny room that felt smaller than it ever had before—like the walls were constricting, closing in around him— how was he supposed to go on with life? How was he supposed to face Lisa and pretend to be a good man, someone worthy of her love? How was he supposed to show up at work like he did every day and act like it was the same as every day before it? Inside that laundry room, with an enraged father on the other side of that sickly, peeling, rusty door, Alice had died.

And Roger might as well have died with her.

"DEAR GOD. Roger, that's awful. You could call Kara, but not 9-1-1? I understand sitting there with the screaming and yelling, but sitting there while a child dies in front of you?"

"I told you your opinion of me would change," Roger said with a snort. "I didn't know she was asthmatic. I'd never seen her with an inhaler. I never saw her have an attack until that moment. I didn't know. God help me, I didn't know."

Mark frowned, more at his own outburst than at Roger. His fingers toyed with his beard. "I'm sorry. I can't imagine living with something like that."

Mark understood why Roger thought he would contact the authorities and turn him in, but Mark wouldn't have wanted to go to the police with this story even if he had been able to. He felt like the man had suffered enough for something that was obviously an accident. He could see the trauma it had caused, the pain and scars it had left behind. In all the time Roger had been coming to him, he had never mentioned this story. He had said earlier that he never told anyone. Holding onto something this big, this painful, for so long, had to do real damage to him. It was going to be a long road to repair it, but now that he knew what they were up against, Mark felt they could repair it together. He felt he could help. It was just going to take time and dedication.

He couldn't imagine how he would feel if something like this horrible story had happened to him, and it easily could have. That was probably why he couldn't help but picture himself as he listened to it. Mark wasn't a fighter any more than Roger. His mind and his heart had always been his greatest weapons. He could clearly see in his mind the intimidating nature of the violent, bigger man. He would hate to have been in that situation, with no time to think and simply needing to act. It was a horrible tragedy to say the very least.

"Tell me about it. It still gets worse," Roger huffed. He was fidgeting now as he had described his story. His shaking fingers danced over each other like mating spiders.

"Worse?"

Such a thing didn't even seem possible to Mark at this point. How could this story get any worse than being trapped in little more than a closet with the body of a dead child, the child you tried to save?

Roger just shook his head. "Much worse."

Roger let out a long exhale and directed his eyes toward the window, as if he needed the sunlight to cast away some of his personal darkness. "It's hard to believe that a story like this, a memory, could even exist in daylight. I almost thought telling it for the first time would make the sun blink out and cast the world into blackness. Especially now. I feel bad for dragging you into these shadows with me, but I couldn't bear the weight of them any longer by myself. I'm sorry if that's selfish. It probably doesn't matter anyhow. Any bit of me that was a good person died in that laundry room with Alice."

There was a pause. The room hung in thick silence. Mark knew that he should fix it, say something, but his own mind was reeling. He couldn't imagine what could be worse than what he had already heard. All he could do was wait with bated breath for what was to come.

Roger inhaled deeply. When he released it, it dragged on,

almost whistling, like a haunting wind had entered the room. You could have heard a pin drop when the last of his breath left his lips. Then he continued.

"When I realized that something was wrong, I panicked. I cried, but I still tried to remain quiet. As shameful as it is, I was still afraid for my own safety."

Roger bit his lips against a silent scream that reddened his face. He thought maybe it wasn't over. Maybe Alice wasn't dead. Maybe her fit had just rendered her unconscious. He couldn't accept that this was happening, that with the terrifying, abusive father she survived every day, Roger had managed to be the one to kill her in his effort to save her.

He tried to wake her, to revive her, to bring her back. Roger did CPR, but his knowledge of it came from movies and TV rather than any real classes. He felt like he probably just made things worse, did more damage, but what else could he do? He had to at least try to save her. He had to do something other than just sit there in the laundry room staring at the frozen, blue-tinted face of the child he quite possibly had a hand in killing.

He breathed into her small pale lips, compressing her chest, trying all he knew how to do, but he was still far too afraid to go back out into that hall and to admit to the man that waited out there what he had done. He wouldn't have had the courage to admit that kind of guilt to the average parent, never mind such a violent and terrifying brute of a man like Brian. Roger couldn't face this. He couldn't even face it when he looked within himself. It couldn't be real. He mouthed the words as he looked down at the still, blue form of the child.

Roger couldn't face the fact that he had killed a child. His mind refused to comprehend such a terrible thing. It was not something he was capable of. Worse still, it was a child who had already been so victimized. Roger was a good man. Maybe not the bravest man, but a good man, nonetheless. He was not a fighter. He was not a *killer*. He was not able to accept this reality at all, but he had to, because it was real. He did it. He was living this horror. There was no escaping it, as much as he desperately wanted to. Roger had killed the child he had been trying to save. That was his truth, his dark and terrible truth.

He waited there in that laundry room, the dead girl in his arms growing colder and stiffer by the moment, until her father finally took off and abandoned the floor. Most likely, he left the building to go look for her outside. Whatever the reason, Roger was relieved. When he heard the bear's trampling footsteps and the receding sound of his voice calling for Alice as he descended the stairwell, door slamming behind him, Roger finally breathed. His eyes found the girl's doll lying beside her now open hand and he cried. His whole body shook with the sobs that racked him. He knew he should be moving, running, escaping before Brian returned, but he couldn't. He couldn't stop the overwhelming grief and guilt that ate away at him like sulfuric acid. He just apologized over and over, shaking and crying as he did.

Dr. Mark Stephenson blinked away tears, his heart feeling heavy. "I'm pretty sure anyone would have been scared and remorseful in that situation, Roger. I can honestly admit to you I would have been. I can't even imagine what you felt like in that moment. This is the most tragic story I have heard in a very long time. I'm so sorry that you had to go through that."

Roger stared at him for a moment. "Don't be sorry for me. Be sorry for Alice. Maybe you would have felt guilty and scared, but you wouldn't have done what I did next. I'm sure of that. It was such a terrible, cowardly thing."

"Roger, what did you do?"

"Not knowing what else to do, I scooped her up, and I ran."

Alice's doll remained alone on the floor distanced from her limp hand as he picked her up in his arms. He left the dirty old thing laying in the laundry room, just as Alice had been laying there, unmoving and staring up at the ceiling but seeing nothing. He couldn't bring himself to go back for it, to touch it with his own hands.

Roger carried the girl in his arms to the elevator. He kicked the down button with his foot. He took the elevator to the second floor. He didn't want to run into Alice's father in the stairwell, especially with the girl in his arms. He also didn't want to run into him in the lobby. He didn't want to run into anyone for that matter while he was carrying a dead child in his arms. What could be more damning than that?

When he got to the second floor, Roger made sure the coast was clear before stepping out of the elevator. There was a girl he liked who lived on this floor. She was now the luckiest girl in the world that he never had the courage to talk to her. Still, he was glad to see she wasn't in the hall. He ran down the stairwell at the back of the building, racing through the dark of the parking garage, his heart thundering so hard he felt it pulsating in his ears. He felt sure someone was going to see him, to report what they saw. His chest constricted like a python was wrapped around him, squeezing the breath out of him with its serpentine embrace.

When he got to the car, he was thankful no one saw him or at least *he* hadn't seen anyone. He didn't hear any conversations or footsteps. By all accounts, it seemed like he was alone down there. It was a stroke of luck on the worst day of his life. He wished some of that luck had been Alice's. He looked down at her lifeless face, eyes still wide open and distressed. Sadness almost dropped him to the pavement in the dank garage. He opened his car door with shaking hands and placed her down as gently as he could. Then those same shaking fingers closed her eyes.

"Don't look at me," he said quietly. "I'm so sorry."

Roger covered her with a blanket he had in his trunk, his paranoia making him look around constantly as he opened the trunk and went to retrieve it. When he laid the blanket over her, he did it in a nurturing way, like he was putting her to bed. He didn't cover her face. He would never cover her face again. That was what got them here. Roger wasn't trying to hide her from prying eyes with the blanket, to obscure the evidence of his crime. It was insane, even to him, but he still felt like he needed to take care of her, make sure she was comfortable. She felt so cold to the touch. A blanket seemed the right thing to do. Grief wasn't always rational.

Roger's quivering hands took three tries to get the key in the ignition. Once the car was in motion, Roger rushed her to the ER, apologizing the whole way and asking for her forgiveness as he drove. He talked to her about what he thought was going to happen, and how it went all wrong and he begged her to under-stand, to see his intentions. He didn't know if the dead could hear the living, but his conscience made him try.

When he got there, Roger was afraid to tell the triage nurse the truth, even though it was truly an accident. He didn't think they would believe his innocence. They didn't live at Sunnycrest.

They didn't see the way Brian treated his daughter or hear the screaming and stomping that was enough to chase Lisa away. They would see Roger as the guilty party, even though his heart knew the blame fell on Brian.

Roger was afraid of going to prison. He knew they would chew him up and spit him out in there. He wasn't built for that kind of life. He couldn't even face Brian in the hallway. How could he deal with violent offenders that wanted to hurt him? He wouldn't stand a chance. It may be what he deserved, he told himself, but he wasn't strong enough to willingly put himself through it even if that were the case.

Imagining prison and how alone he would be made him loathe himself even more and see himself as more of a coward than the day's events had already shown him to be: a child killer. There would be nowhere to hide, no one to save him, no one that would even care to. It would be hell. Movies played in his mind of himself in a jumpsuit being beaten by similarly dressed people while the guards watched and laughed. Then they joined in with their nightsticks, and he could feel his bones breaking. Roger shook his head like it was an Etch-a-sketch and he needed to erase what his mind had drawn.

Just thinking about it, imagining it in his anxious mind, made him want to vomit. The only reason he didn't was because he wanted to get out of the hospital without incident. He knew he needed to tell them something though, so he did, but he left out the part that he had stolen that precious child's final breaths from her with his silencing hand. He didn't lie, but he didn't really tell them the whole truth either. What he did tell, he told through very real tears and anxious hyperventilating breaths.

Roger told the nurses that he found her in the hallway and he knew by the sight of her that something was wrong. He told them he had heard her father abusing her, not just that day, but frequently. He mentioned his girlfriend wouldn't even come by because the sounds of the man's anger were so frightening and disturbing to her.

Through his sobs, he said, "I heard him screaming in the apartment and breaking things when I found her laying there. I was afraid if I called for an ambulance, he would do something with her before they arrived. I was also afraid if I stayed by her that he would do something to me. I was so scared. There is something *evil* in that man, like he's possessed by a demon. I know I should have called the police a long time ago. I should have gotten her help. This is my fault as well, because I went on with life and did nothing to save her from that animal. Oh my god, I'm so sorry. I'm just so sorry." Roger's words were genuine. Then he apologized to them if he had done the wrong thing and messed up a crime scene. "Please don't tell me that monster is going to get away with this. Tell me he's not going to get away with it and it's not my fault for messing everything up."

The nurses assured him, just like he had assured Alice, that it would be alright. Just like him, they had no idea how completely wrong they were. The hospital called the police, and Roger sat in a hardbacked, bright-colored chair, rocking back and forth and wiping his nose with his forearm while making no effort to stop his tears. They gave him a heated blanket and a cup of water.

After the police talked to the nurses, they came to Roger for his statement. He allowed them to search his car, and Roger said he would do anything they needed, anything to help. His eyes were red with heavy bags under them. Roger told them the same thing he told the nurses. He was even able to give them specific dates because he remembered his fights with Lisa, another thing Brian's anger ruined.

He threw Alice's father under the bus with everything he had to save his own hide. The whole time he felt like someone was going to call him on his bullshit. Someone was going to demand he stop lying. He imagined all the possible scenarios in his head and pictured policemen screaming just like Brian had, with red faces, spittle flying, and thick index fingers jabbing at the air in front of his face. He was waiting to be accused, but he never was. The hammer never came down.

The police officers were sad, had families of their own, and thanked him for what he had done. Apparently there had been prior complaints on Alice's father, just nothing that stuck. Their supportive hands on Roger's shoulders, the water they kept refilling for him, and the soft way they spoke to him was evidence that they sympathized with him. One officer even said to him, "Even if it was too late, at least someone finally took care of her. Taking care of her in death when no one did in life. We all should have done something before today, not just you. We all failed this little girl."

Roger almost threw up then, but he swallowed it down and grimaced at the horrible acidic taste it left in his mouth. He heard their gratitude and he almost boiled over and confessed.

Almost, but he didn't.

He knew his motivations were entirely selfish. He justified it in his mind. He wasn't trying to make a bad man pay for the terrible way he treated an innocent child. Roger was trying to not take the fall for something he would always know in his heart he was guilty of, regardless of what anyone else thought. Brian *was* bad though, wasn't he? He did scream and yell and break things. He was overly aggressive if nothing else. Brain deserved to go to prison, didn't he? Whether Brian did or he didn't deserve to go, Roger knew that he himself definitely deserved to do time behind bars for his crime, accident or not. That was just one more thing he was going to have to live with.

Mark shook his head. He pushed his seat back and stood. Then, he walked around the desk and gave his patient a supportive pat on the shoulder before moving to the window and opening it, taking a big inhale of the fresh air The room felt stuffy now, and his collar felt too tight. Fresh air was a saving grace. He wasn't supposed to get emotional, but it was hard not to, listening to stories like that. Abuse and children being hurt brought back his own trauma. It took several deep breaths to put it back in its box so he could focus on his job and his patient.

"I honestly don't know why I said it, why I avoided the truth so adamantly," Roger told his doctor, wiping tears from his eyes. Mark imagined him crying the same way as he stood in the laundry room on that terrible day. Roger scratched at his stubbled chin. "I don't know why I did anything I did that day. I really don't. I was flying by the seat of my pants, just doing and doing, never stopping to think about any of it, other than the terrible thoughts anxiety gave me. Everything happened so fast. It was so damned fast, Mark. I guess it doesn't really matter now, does it? The end result was that I was the murderer, and yet I was hailed as a good Samaritan who came up short, while Alice's father was found guilty of negligence and manslaughter. He was put behind bars even though hadn't actually killed anyone. I'm scum, plain and simple."

Mark looked back at the nervous man sitting before his desk, fidgeting. "I can't believe you held this all in. I wish you had felt comfortable enough to tell this story months ago, so we could have been working through this together all this time. This is way too much for anyone to handle alone, Roger. Even if you had gone to jail, I could have still had sessions with you. I've worked with prisoners in the past."

Roger snapped to attention and stared at him after hearing the word "alone." It was like he had seen a ghost, but then it passed. His tense shoulders relaxed, and he slouched, looking defeated. He took a deep breath and said, "I really am tired of hiding. I told you so I could be unburdened. Just call the police. I'll wait right here. That does sound good, you still talking to me when I'm in there. Please follow through on that."

Mark Stephenson sighed and sat on the edge of his desk. He shook his head. "Let's not jump to that. There's a lot to take in and process here. Let's try to take some time to do that, okay?"

Roger nodded. His eyes fluttered around the room, searching the shadows for something or someone. He shifted in his seat as if he were avoiding something.

The doctor frowned again and followed it with an exasperated sigh. Images of his own troubled past started to form in his mind. He shut his eyes and waited for them to pass. Then he opened them back up and did his best to force a smile. He felt sick, but he didn't want Roger to see that. He slapped his hands down on his thighs. "Sometimes, you try to do the right thing, and it doesn't work out like you want it to." His mind showed him a brown-haired boy in a red shirt, and he blinked it away. "That whole situation is horrible, truly terrible, Roger. I can't say that I would have done differently, not if I'm truly being honest with you. I'm so sorry that you had to go through that, Roger. I am just so sorry."

"Me?" Roger seemed almost offended, annoyed by his doctor's empathy. "What about Alice? What about the child I killed who hasn't seen justice? I could change it, but I'm too much of a coward to turn myself in, so just do it. Just call the police and tell them what I've told you. End this once and for all. Do it!"

Mark frowned once again. "Roger, I don't want to do that, and I don't think you really want me to do that, at least, not just yet, okay? You've had this secret eating away at you like a cancer for what? A year now? Let's try to deal with those feelings now, and take some time to try to find a way to heal from this. If you decide then you want to turn yourself in, then I will help you do that, but let's not be rash. Rash behavior is what created this situation, right? So, let's do something different this time. For now, let's focus on you, because there's nothing you can do now to bring Alice back. She...wait." Something occurred to Mark.

"You started this conversation by telling me that Alice was back. What did you mean by that?"

Roger stood from his seat. "I think it's time for me to go. I know I've been here a while now. I've definitely gone over. I appreciate you giving me the extra time and allowing me to explain, but now I... I just need to leave and let you get home to your probably angry wife. I'll see you next week."

Dr. Stephenson stood as well. "Roger, I told you that I'm not worried about that. Please tell me what you meant when you said Alice is back. I need to know what you meant by that, as a friend, not a doctor. Please."

"What do you think I meant?" Roger snapped.

"Are you saying you've been seeing her ghost?" Mark stared intensely at his patient. He felt like he had grown as haggard as Roger had been when the meeting started. This had been an exhausting session. Mark wasn't sure he believed in ghosts, but there were definitely things—things that had seemed strange to say the least—with some of his other patients from Sunnycrest. He thought of Maria. It was hard for him to argue against ghosts after what happened with her.

"I'll see you next week," Roger answered, then he made his way out and closed the door behind him.

Once he was gone, Dr. Mark Stephenson took his glasses off and rested them on his desk. He rubbed his eyes for a minute, surprised they still held some tears. He pressed the button on the intercom to contact his secretary in the next room. He was glad she was flexible and hung around on days like this when he went over. Mark honestly didn't know what he would do without her. Jessica was a godsend. When she answered the page, Mark said, "Sorry for the delay, Jess. Let's go home. I've got a date with a bottle of Scotch."

"Sounds good, Doc," she said back. Then she opened the door and leaned into the room, causing him to laugh and hang up the phone. She had her coat on and her purse over her shoulder.

"Tina Weathers called while you were in there with Roger. She needs you to call in a refill for her meds."

Mark nodded. "Thanks, Jess. I should check how Roger's meds are doing while I'm at it. You go on. I'll lock up. See you tomorrow."

Jessica gave a salute and then eased out and let the door fall gently closed. With a sigh, Mark picked the phone back up.

5

ROGER HEADED to the street after leaving the doctor's office. Standing just inside the curb, he started trying to hail a cab. He hated needing to do so. He hated the city all together, the hustle and bustle, the filth, the constant noise, all of it. Roger had grown up in a small residential community in mid-western suburbia, where everyone drove everywhere because there was nothing in walking distance, and they lived quiet lives. They worked and took care of their families. That was the gist of it. Of course, Kara grew up there too and she couldn't wait to get away from it, to find something more exciting. Once she left, the small-town life felt a little too quiet for Roger. Kara was the energy that brought that place to life. It seemed like a ghost town without her. So, he took a leap. If only he had known it would lead him to this, to Alice. His stomach lurched with the sickness of guilt.

Sunnycrest was Roger's first apartment here in the city. As far as he was concerned, it would also be his last. If he could ever get free of Alice, then he would break free of this city altogether. Everything here made him think of Lisa, and his heart constantly ached. He would see the Black Widow T-shirt she always wore hanging in shop windows, at the comic shop that had the table at the convention where they met, at the pizza place where they had their first real date, or in the shop where she bought her custom-made, high-heeled Converse high-tops. It made him wish he were anywhere else in the world.

He couldn't leave though. He couldn't even leave the building, never mind the city. If Alice was tethered to this world, unable to let go and move on, it was because of unfinished business or unresolved feelings, and he was the source of them, the thing that kept her chained to the mortal world. He already took her life, accidentally or not. He couldn't handle being the reason her soul never reached heaven on top of it. Sunnycrest was the thing that tethered him to her. If he broke his bond, then she may never be able to break hers. It left him stuck, afraid, and hating life.

He reminded himself that he had no one else to blame. Except, he did blame someone else. Maybe it was wrong, but he still blamed Brian. That day wouldn't have happened if Alice's father hadn't been such a monster to begin with. Roger thought it was really all Brian's fault, and then thinking that way made him feel like a coward and a terrible person all over again. It was a vicious cycle. Welcome to the world of anxiety, he thought with a huff.

Roger was more than ready to leave it all behind and go back home, back to the quiet of his parent's home, or maybe somewhere else entirely. He could go somewhere even more remote and rural, where he would be the only living person, not that he wanted to bring the dead with him either. Roger was beginning to think after this that there was no such thing as too quiet. Kara could keep her hustle and bustle and thrive here, and he could write her from his cabin in the woods a million miles away. But first, he had to find a way to free Alice. To free Alice was to free himself. He owed it to her, even if he was terrified of her, and he owed it to himself not to drag this kind of weight through the rest of his life.

Roger always thought about the future, about escaping. He chalked it up to his cowardice that he found happiness in running away, but thinking about a way out helped him to get through the present. Mark had told him it was okay as long as it was just a coping mechanism, and he didn't follow through with it. He suggested Roger keep a journal or a scrapbook with all the places he would like to go and things he would like to do. It was great advice.

One day, he would leave this all behind, Alice included, and go to one of the places cut from a magazine and paste in said scrapbook. In the meantime, his guilt held him in place like an anchor. Until he could conquer it, he couldn't go anywhere, and he didn't even know if conquering it was something he could do. He had to at least try, though the last time he tried to save someone, it went horribly wrong. He hoped saving himself would go better. If it didn't, would he deserve any better? How would Alice answer that question? She was the only one who truly could.

As he searched the streets for a taxi, Roger continued to think about his life since leaving the suburban calm for the chaos of the big city. He thought of Lisa. He wished she had hung around and been there to support him through this, but she wouldn't have anyway, would she? She had already been so judgmental of him and how he handled things with Brian and that whole situation. The full truth would send her swan diving over the edge. Lisa would have turned him in, added to his suffering, then left him without a qualm. Knowing the truth of this only served to break his heart further. How had it all gone so wrong?

He bit his lip and wondered if he had been rash by running out before his Mark had actually cut him loose. If anyone could help him, it was Mark Stephenson, who just instructed him not to be rash. He should have changed the subject from Alice to Lisa. Lisa had left him before Alice left the world.

Roger would never forget the way she cut him loose. He had been heading up the front walkway to Sunnycrest when a strange boy stopped him.

The boy had said, "I'm supposed to give you these," and handed Roger a bouquet of roses and a *Nightbreed* first edition.

Before Roger could say anything, the boy rollerskated away, a ten-dollar bill dangling from his fist. Roger scoffed. *Who's the coward now?*

Even after that rude break up, Roger still loved Lisa, but now that he thought about it, he couldn't figure out why. Why had he fought so hard to hold on to her? Maybe he just couldn't handle being alone. Maybe that was why he felt inclined to follow Kara too. Everything fell back to his own personal weakness. He sighed and waved at a taxi, but it sped by and splashed muddy water from a nearby puddle onto his pant leg. His shoulders slumped. He considered turning back, seeing if Mark was still there and still willing to talk to him.

Mark had seemed supportive, but that was his job. Roger had no way to know for sure what Mark thought of him or the story he had told the man. He did seem to get angry with Roger at one point. It was fleeting but maybe it was a glimpse of his true feelings. Roger had always felt like everyone hated him deep down, and it made him push people away. That was another side of life with anxiety.

He did his best to brush off the thought and convince himself that Mark's care was real. He had seen the tears in the man's eyes and heard the empathy in his voice. Roger didn't know why, but his gut said Mark was actually there to help him. The real question was, could he really be helped? He certainly didn't feel like it. He supposed time would tell, though sometimes he wondered how much time he really had. How much time did he have before Alice stopped toying with him and finally took her revenge? If that was what it would take for her to move on to heaven, would he even stop her? He had more questions than answers.

Where the hell were the taxis today? Usually the overpriced cars were everywhere, ushering people back and forth across the flat city like it was a basketball court, but today they were few and far between. He must have used up all his luck escaping prison the day Alice died.

It made Roger's flesh bead up with the perspiration of stress as his anxiety deepened. He was in a hurry to get off the street, out of the open, and back to his home, though he didn't quite understand why. He had good reason to believe Alice would be there waiting for him. Was his mental illness so bad that the company of a ghost was more desirable than being amongst strangers in public? *Maybe so*, he admitted.

It was becoming a regular occurrence, a part of his everyday life. Her presence was beginning to seem as normal and routine as the couch and bed. She was becoming a fixture. Maybe he was tethered to the building more than he realized and he was stretching the leash too far. Roger didn't know what to believe but his anxiety would be sure to raise plenty of questions. It always did, even when he was trying to work or sleep. He remembered what it had been like before he left his apartment this morning.

Roger stared at the articles of clothing that were strewn about the apartment. He felt so defeated as he looked at them. He shook his head in disgust. He was out of clean clothes. His dirty items weren't even piled or organized. Once the hamper had become full to the point of spilling over onto the floor around it like the eruption of a fabric-filled volcano, he started tossing clothing everywhere. Who did he have to impress with Lisa gone? It didn't matter. Roger exhausted every article of clothing in his possession. Some of them weren't appropriate for the office where he worked, but he had put off doing laundry since Alice had started showing up more. He told himself that he could use the other laundry room, but he feared the outcome wouldn't be any different. He didn't know if that was rational or not, but whether it was or wasn't didn't change anything for him. He felt terrified of going into that laundry room, or any other, of entering the type of place where it all happened. His mind had never really left that laundry room for the past year. As he stared at the gray sweatshirt at his feet, Roger's mind filled with images of Alice's still form on the laundry room floor, pale hand opening to release that filthy doll that he left there to die as well, her empty eyes staring up at nothing. He shivered and covered his mouth as bile rose into his throat. His shot nerves had brought him reflux that didn't help anything. Roger silently mouthed the words, *I'm sorry*, as tears rose in his eyes.

When the daydream faded and reality returned, the room held a chill that made Roger hug himself. He exhaled and marveled at the fact he could see his breath like a plume of smoke in the air before him. He paused and listened carefully. He could hear the hum of the central heating blowing through the vents in the floors and walls. Roger shook his head slowly. It shouldn't be as cold as it was. It wasn't natural. He knew what it was though—or rather *who* it was. He didn't need anyone to tell him Alice was in the room with him, even if he couldn't see her.

A whispering came through the unnatural breeze, finding its way into his ear. He couldn't make it out. The words were garbled, backwards maybe. They sounded strange and distant as if they were struggling to reach him through a tunnel. Could there be a pathway between her world and his? Roger shivered again and hugged himself tighter.

He didn't know what else to do, so he just stood there and waited to see what was going to happen. The whispers faded away, and the chill dropped off. In a few moments, Roger was left standing in his mess of a laundry-covered bedroom, wondering if any of it had been real or if it had been lingering aftershocks from his daydream. He sighed, his heart heavy with the stress of guilt.

Roger knew he had to do laundry, but he didn't feel like he could, especially after what had just happened. He felt like it would bring him crashing back to that moment and start it all over again, forcing him to relive it on a loop like a horrible Groundhog's Day, and he couldn't bear to do it even one more time. Being trapped in that horrible moment would be Roger's personal version of hell. He couldn't help but wonder if that was what was waiting for him when he did eventually die. Either way, he was not crazy enough to walk into the fire willingly, at least not yet.

Roger considered packing a bag of clothes and taking them somewhere else to wash, that maybe it would be better outside of this building, but he stood outside the laundromat one day and couldn't handle the idea of being in there. He stared through the glass front. There were so many people packed into a small space and rolling tumbling machines endlessly banging away off rhythm to each other, a cacophony of chaos. It smelled like a potpourri blend of flowers, trash, and laundry soap, which sickened his stomach even standing outside the open front door. He didn't think his anxiety would let him do it, not for the hours it took to complete. He was sensitive to sounds and smells, easily bothered by such things. All the more reason this city was the wrong place for him. At least once a day, he wished he had just stayed home. Everyone probably wished for a time machine though, didn't they? Chastising himself for the bad choices that led him here wasn't going to get his clothes clean.

Roger shook his head. No. If he called his sister, he was sure Kara would let him go over to her place and wash his clothes there, and for free, but she was a worry wart. She seemed to forget she was his sister and *not* his mother. It had always been that way. When he was younger, he needed it, but as they got older, she never really let him break away. *Look at yourself, Rodge. Did you ever really stop needing it?*

Their actual mother was quite the opposite of his worrisome sister. She wanted them to learn about life and said the best way to do so was through experience, so she took a step back and allowed them to live, standing by and watching them make mistakes. She had this amazing way of justifying negligence. He should probably talk to Mark about that at some point.

Roger remembered when he had tried to climb a motel sign and he had fallen hard, breaking his arm. It was his sister and her usual frown that came to pick him up and take him to the hospital. They had to rebreak it before they could set it. It was a horrible experience he would never forget. He would also remember that his mother was there, watching him as he climbed and fell. He would never forget her casually shaking her head at him as he screamed in agony, clutching at his splintered bones that stuck through his shredded flesh.

"Well, you won't do that again, will you?" she had said. "Now you've learned. Remember this moment; remember how it feels. Remember and grow. This is an important moment for you, Roger."

Kara was only three years older but always looked after Roger and did her best to make sure he was always okay. For the most part, she succeeded, and he was grateful to her for all she had done, even though her worrying sometimes drove him crazy, which was what made him hesitant now. She would want to know why he was so afraid, why he hadn't done laundry in so long, and it would spiral into his eating habits and sleeping habits and whether or not he was taking his meds, how his job was going, if he was getting back out there after Lisa, and everything else under the sun. He felt anxious just thinking about it and wiped sweat from the back of his neck.

Roger decided he should probably avoid his sister for a while, at least until he found some way to get himself under control, or at least to a point where she wouldn't freak out at the sight of him, disheveled with dark rings circling his bloodshot, sleep-deprived eyes. He could just hear her. "Have you been sleeping? What's going on? Why can't you use the laundry room at your place? Are you over tired or did somebody hit you? It looks like you have black eyes, Rodge! Have you been eating? Talk to me.

What's going on? You haven't missed work, have you? I can't afford to help you with rent right now."

Maybe Mark would help him get himself together. Roger had an appointment with his psychiatrist today. Soon actually. He chewed on his nails as he looked at the clock. He needed to leave now. He was going to be late, and it made his heart quicken. Roger made the decision to just go to his appointment wearing the clothes he had been in for two days. He needed to hurry.

Roger thought about what had just happened, about the visit. He decided that today was the day. He would tell Mark the truth, confess about Alice. Even if Mark couldn't help him, maybe telling the story finally would be enough for Alice to forgive him. He would find out soon enough.

As he hurried out of his apartment, he could hear the whispering voice of a child. He froze for a moment and strained to listen, but the words didn't reach him. The breath caught in his chest. He locked his door and turned around to find a familiar filthy doll laying in the hall at his feet. Roger looked down the hallway in both directions but saw no one. He didn't need any help hurrying to the elevator and out of Sunnycrest after that. His feet couldn't go fast enough as far as he was concerned. Even as he fled through the front doors of the building, he thought he could still hear that tiny voice carried on the breeze, trying to reach him.

ROGER HAD CONFESSED as he had planned to, but he had also run away, as he was adept at doing. He couldn't deal with the stress of hanging around to see how the dust settled with the good Dr. Stephenson. It was too much for him.

One step at a time, he told himself as he wiped sweat from his forehead with clammy hands. He could deal with Mark's reaction later or the doctor would call if he couldn't wait until next week. Roger didn't like talking to the doctor on the phone. It felt far less comfortable than talking in person for some reason. He preferred when Mark stuck to calling in his prescriptions and waited to see him at his scheduled appointment time. Right now, he needed to find a damn taxi and get home.

He was beginning to have an anxiety attack out here on the street, his chest seizing like someone was standing on it and refusing to let up so he could breathe. Panic was rising within him as he struggled for breath. Roger felt like everyone was staring at him, although he knew it was probably all in his mind. He could hear their inner monologues discussing his strange behavior.

"What's with him?"

"Look at him sweating so much. Disgusting. It's not even warm. There's something wrong with him. I wonder if it's contagious."

"Guy is some kind of freak, panicking like he killed somebody or something."

"Maybe he did."

"Weirdo."

"Maybe he's one of those apocalyptic nuts."

Knowing anxiety was irrational didn't turn it off. Part of the symptom list was the inability to shut his brain off. His own inner voice projected endlessly. It was as damning as the false voices of the surrounding public that plagued him, if not more so. Roger got antsy and started tugging at his collar, needing space around his neck as the constriction of his chest rose to his throat. His mouth was dry, and it felt hard to swallow. *Where were all the damned taxis in this city? Please! Come on already!*

Roger clawed at his clothes, ready to rip his shirt off out there in the street, when a yellow cab at last slowed down and pulled over toward the curb in front of him. He closed his eyes and sighed with relief, then he stretched his tired muscles. Silently, he thanked God, though he didn't believe God was ever truly listening.

When the taxi pulled itself to a complete stop, Roger took the necessary couple of steps to the back driver's side door. Seizing the handle, he started to open it, but hesitated. Fear gripped his guilt-ridden heart like a cold steel vice. He was sweating profusely now, blinking it away as it stung his eyes. The weight on his chest increased and stopped his breath completely.

Looking out at him through the back window was a young girl who sat inside the cab next to the door. Her once beautiful, long, black locks hung about her head like strings of seaweed. Branches of hair like the clawing hands of a diseased tree dangled in front of her small face. Her skin, so pale it bordered on blue was mottled with black and yellow bruises. Veins scrawled across her sunken cheeks like strikes of black lightning. Her eyes were as dark as coal, and their stare was intense and full of hatred, and they pinpoint focused right on him.

Roger recognized Alice immediately, despite the differences

in her appearance. When he saw her at home, she had looked as she had in life, a reminder of the innocence he had stolen from the world. This version of her had clearly been dead the whole time and, judging by the intensity of her stare, she was angry.

Roger released the door handle and backed up a step, stumbling as his heel caught the curb. Staring back at her, he tried to calm himself with deep breaths but his limbs trembled in fright. Why was she here? Why was she like *that*?

Ever so slowly, a smile crawled across Alice's pallid face. Roger's breath was still unobtainable. He felt like he was suffocating. Was it his anxiety or could it have been something more, something she was doing? Was she stealing his breath as he had stolen hers? Roger had no idea what this vengeful child was capable of.

He stumbled backward again and almost tripped and fell, catching himself with a palm to the pavement that he skinned on the gravel and dirt. He had never seen Alice outside the apartment before. He thought she was bound to that menacing building, like the ghosts in the haunted house movies he had seen, but apparently, he was wrong. She was here now in the cab, smiling at him, reveling in his suffocation. Roger could only stare at the dead child with quivering eyes full of terror.

"You getting in or not?" the driver snapped, displaying annoyance with his gruff tone.

"Huh?" Roger said, turning to face the overweight bald man in a stained wife beater tank top behind the steering wheel that had pushed itself into his belly.

Out of the corner of his eye, Roger could still see Alice staring and smiling from the backseat, no smile in her eyes. Did this guy not even know she was there in the car with him? Could he not see her in his rearview mirror? Was he unaware his taxi was currently being requisitioned by a non-paying passenger from somewhere far outside the city?

Roger shook his head. "Um...no. That's okay. I'm sorry. I think I'll walk. I'm sorry to bother you."

The driver called Roger a freak—just like the voices in his head—as Roger hurried away from the taxi and rushed down the street, wanting nothing more than to put distance between himself and the car's unknown passenger. Her laughter trailed after him as he scrambled to get away. It sounded like the notes of childish glee were following him like footsteps. He felt like the sound of her would grab him like audible fingers and drag him back to the taxi, pulling him inside and driving him to Hell. He would have screamed if he could have found the breath to do so.

Roger was trying to deal with the realization that Alice could leave Sunnycrest just like he could. How had she so casually ventured out after him? What else was she capable of? Did she have any limitations? How far was her reach? His anxiety only increased with this line of thought. If she didn't succeed in driving him mad, he was going to do it himself.

Roger couldn't catch his breath, and his skin crawled like there were a million little invisible spiders running all over his body, scurrying across the bony flesh hidden beneath his now baggy unwashed clothes. He didn't slow down. He couldn't slow down, not until he was sure that he was far enough away and he had put a good deal of distance between him and the taxi that was unaware it had become a hearse.

Roger didn't care what the driver thought of him. That was the least of his problems. He was much more intimidated by Alice than he was anyone in the living world, at least in this moment. He was starting to see spots and stumble drunkenly as he moved along, in desperate need for oxygen that he couldn't find. The idea of passing out on the sidewalk and leaving himself vulnerable to Alice or the human vermin that patrolled the streets in search of easy prey heightened his anxiety even more. He started envisioning all the awful possibilities and the more anxious he got, the more he couldn't breathe. He was no longer running. He couldn't. His legs felt like lead weights without the oxygen they needed.

Roger finally stopped in his tracks. He tried hard to get a hold of himself. He had to. His heart raced and those phantom arachnids were making him want to scratch at himself like a wild man. He fought the urge, knowing he would look even crazier than he already did. It was conflicting to not care about what people thought, but also care about it completely at the same time.

Bending over, Roger panted and coughed as he worked desperately to try to catch his breath. He felt like he was choking, like a ghostly hand had a hold of his throat, but he knew this had nothing to do with Alice. This was the hand of anxiety. It was a different type of haunting that followed him through life just as relentlessly—maybe more so—and had for as long as he could remember.

"You okay?" a woman asked him, stopping nearby with a concerned look on her overly made up face. Through his half blind eyes struggling to maintain their hold on consciousness, she looked like a sad clown.

It was unusual for city folk to be at all concerned with the goings-on around them, beyond passing judgment. This random gesture of kindness took Roger by surprise. He realized then he must have really looked as troubled as he felt for these apathetic people to notice him, to know this time it wasn't merely in his head. It made him feel self-conscious and sent his anxiety into overdrive, his eyes moving past the woman and roaming over all the others. There were so many. There always were. The city was packed like a sardine can. It stayed that way, all hours of every day. Internally, Roger screamed his head off.

Externally, he grit his teeth against the pain stabbing into his chest. His muscles screamed as the invisible hand of his mental illness squeezed them like the fist of a God. He felt like he was going to die there on the street. What would happen then? Would Alice come get him to take him to Hell? Would she be waiting for him in the afterlife? What would she have in store for him then? Would those horrors last for eternity?

He couldn't think about it. He had to get himself under control. *For God's sake, you have to breathe.*

His legs felt weak, unable to hold him up much longer. It felt like someone was jamming knitting needles into his pectorals.

Roger looked at the stranger's face and tried not to grimace at the fact she had enough paint decorating her features to fit in with a traveling circus. He could see the way it filled and clogged her pores and it made him nauseous, but she was being kind to him. He couldn't be rude in response. Roger forced a smile then, wondering what it looked like from the other side, how believable it really was. He imagined he looked like the Cheshire cat.

"Yeah. Yeah, I'm good. Thanks. Thank you," he croaked awkwardly.

"Alright," the stranger said.

She walked away but not without paying him one last concerned glance. Roger made sure to smile again to reassure her. He stood there for a moment, still working on catching his breath, and listened to the sound of the woman's high heels clicking away at the pavement as she left. It was just what he needed.

Roger focused on the sound, homing in on it until everything else was gone from his mind. The street, the people, the cars, and the city itself were gone. There was nothing around but him and the metronome-like, rhythmic clicking of the woman's heels on the concrete.

Tap. Tap. Tap. Tap.

Roger's heart slowed down and his breathing became more regular. Mark had taught him that trick to relieve an anxiety attack during one of their previous sessions. It had done him well so far. Anytime he felt himself having a panic attack, he found a sight or sound to focus on, usually something with a rhythm, and he glued himself to it until he regained self-control. He thought about how often he had already made use of that tool, and he wondered if it was the reason he felt so inclined to trust the man. At least one thing the doctor had given him proved to be true and for his benefit. The proof was in the pudding as they say.

As air started to move through his lungs once more and his blood flowed as seamlessly as it should, returning feeling to his limbs, Roger thought about his only time going to the circus as a child.

Ten-year-old Roger was nervous. He had been excited about going to the circus when his mother had said she had gotten tickets, but now that they'd arrived, he felt overwhelmed. There were so many people and large, looming tents. One man towered over everyone on impossibly long legs that bent awkwardly in an inhuman way. Roger was frightened by the man, and he fled, his mother letting him. The more he ran, the more lost and alone he felt and the more his fear increased. This wasn't fun at all.

Roger ducked inside one of the tents, crawling under a flap of canvas in hopes of finding a brief respite from all the frightening things crowding his senses. He found himself surrounded by more disproportionate people wearing stripes and polka dots, their gigantic feet dressed in shining red shoes. They had curly hair of every color in the rainbow and their faces were covered in paint, with smiles painted on even as they stared at him with stern eyes full of judgment. They didn't need to speak to ask him what he was doing there.

Roger looked at the tall, skinny and rotund, wide men that stood all around him, glaring his direction, their lips tight despite the painted smiles that surrounded them. Roger wished his mother was frantically looking for him, that she would come find him, but he knew better. She would wait for him to get back

—if he did—and then ask him about what he learned from the experience.

Roger stumbled backward, his body trembling, and he fell into the tent behind him. Finally, the lips of the surrounding clowns curled into smiles and showed their teeth. A hand clamped down on his shoulder and Roger gasped. He whipped around to see who had a hold of him, and Kara was there, her own smile far more genuine.

"There you are," she said. "Come on."

Roger paid a last glance to the circus performers as his sister took his hand and led him away. He shivered again as he could still feel the judgment in their eyes. His hand tightened on his sister's.

ROGER TOOK a deep breath and felt glad he had never gone back to the circus. The city had its own smaller annual circus that Lisa had wanted to go once, but Roger had quickly declined. He supposed she was free to go to all the circuses she wanted to now.

Changing directions with his thoughts, he considered how interesting it was the way memories were triggered by small details. The kind stranger and her overabundance of makeup connected to the clown trauma from his childhood in his mind. It was odd the way the brain worked.

Then he thought back to that terrible day again and couldn't help but wonder if maybe it had been the catalyst, the trigger that caused the anxiety to stay with him for life. *Thanks, Mom.*

Wiping his face with the back of his hand, Roger took one last deep breath and started off down the street again, feeling much better despite the brief tinge of bitterness with Lisa that left a bad taste in his mouth.

He walked toward home, this time at a leisurely pace, free of worry. Some new music downloaded to his phone would probably do him good. He could listen to music and the rest of the world would just pass him by. Roger would have a constant distraction available for whenever the anxiety decided to rear its ugly head. He would have to keep that in mind for when he got paid on Friday.

Roger had been anxious about listening to music while he walked in the past, afraid he wouldn't hear the dangerous sounds of the city around him, but now his perspective had changed. He could keep his eyes peeled. Now, he felt like his own mind was more of a danger to him than the city.

Would music block out Alice? Or would she be able to overpower it, invade it, and get to him anyway? With this in mind, Roger thought about the day Kara had showed up at his apartment with more Chinese food than the two of them could possibly eat. She had come to cheer him up and convince him to get over Lisa already and get back out there.

"I didn't like her anyway," Kara said with a charming laugh. "There's more women in this city than comic books in your collection, bro. You just have to go out and meet them. I'll be your wing man. Now, I brought the food. Go grab us a couple beers."

Roger nodded and slurped up the remaining lo mein noodles hanging out of his mouth. He wiped his mouth with a napkin, then got to his feet from where they were sitting on the floor in the living room. Kara had insisted on camping on the floor like they had as kids. She wouldn't sit at the table and even went so far as to push his couch back to make more room. Roger cringed at the screech of the wooden legs on the floor, but he didn't protest. Kara knew him well and this probably was what he needed.

Roger returned from the kitchen with two beers in each hand and a bottle opener dangling from the pinky of his right hand and found Kara bent over in front of his TV.

"I have the most basic of basic packages," he told her as he sat on the ground behind her.

"That's fine," she said. "I'm just looking for the music channels since you're the one person in this city with no form of stereo or music player."

She found what she was looking for, and the dance music from their childhood came through the speakers of his television. She increased the volume high enough to annoy his neighbors, which made Roger sweat with anxiety, then she turned around and danced toward him. Smiling wide, Kara snatched a beer from his hand and took a few big gulps as she continued dancing.

"Come on," she said, holding her hand out to him.

Roger wanted to protest, to tell her they needed to lower the volume. He didn't want to be a problem for his neighbors, not when they already had to listen to the commotion of Apartment 33 on a regular basis until he brought that all to an end. He thought about how much quieter the seventh floor had become since Brian's incarceration. He thought about the vacant apartment across the hall that had yet to be rented to anyone else, and the guilt drove him to keep the fridge stocked with beer.

"I can see what you're thinking," Kara said, eyeing him. "Take a sip of that beer and relax. If anyone knocks on the door and complains, we'll lower it and sweetly apologize for bothering them. Until then, get off your ass and start dancing."

Roger sighed. He reached under his pant leg and scratched at his calf. Sometimes anxiety made him itchy. He bit his lip as he thought about the right thing to do.

"Come on," Kara said again, more forcefully.

Roger nodded then. He took a big gulp of beer and stood up. He moved awkwardly, but he started to dance with her.

Kara laughed at him, a deep hearty laugh. "For the love of God, Rodge, lighten up. If you dance like that, you're not going to find a *new* girlfriend."

Roger stopped moving and frowned at her. "That's just mean. Give me a break, Kara."

His sister rolled her eyes and smacked him in the arm, causing some beer to slosh out of the top of his bottle onto the rug. "I said lighten up, not get more uptight. Now, will you please just try to have a good time?"

Roger frowned at the wet spot on the rug, but he didn't dare try to clean it at the moment. He knew Kara would fly all over him for it, especially since it was clear he hadn't done laundry in some time and his bedroom looked the way it did when he was in high school. He took a long deep breath and chugged the rest of his beer and started on his second. Kara was clapping and cheering him on. Roger couldn't help but laugh. He was glad to have her. She'd always been his rock, even when she was far too young to have to deal with that kind of responsibility.

Together they danced to the songs of their childhood, and they laughed and panted for breath. Roger was having fun, real fun, for the first time in a long time. Then he took a break to run to the bathroom and break the seal before retrieving the next round of beers his sister requested. While he was in the bathroom, he stopped to listen. The music from the other room sounded different, strange, and warbled, like it was coming from an old music player with the batteries running out, but that wasn't possible. That wouldn't happen to a television channel.

He wondered if he could be drunk after only two beers. Maybe he drank them too fast. He tried to focus on the music. He knew the song well. It was one of his favorites from middle school. He had never heard it like this. It sounded *wrong*. It was too slow. He wondered if Kara noticed it as well.

Biting his lip against his nerves, Roger washed his hands and headed out of the bathroom. When he got back to the living room with the new beers, the music sounded normal again. The song blared through his television the same way it had sounded for decades. *Weird.* Roger decided it must have sounded strange in the bathroom with the door closed. Maybe it was the acoustics in the apartment or something. He was going to ask Kara if it had sounded strange to her at all while he was gone, but she spoke first.

"Hold that thought," she said, pointing at him. "My turn."

Kara ran off toward the bathroom. Roger called behind her. "Does the music sound strange in there? Is it different at all?"

"Nope," she called back. "Sounds as corny and ridiculous as always."

Roger shrugged. He looked at the beer in his hand wondering if it could truly be the culprit.

Suddenly, the music behind him got strange again. It was slow, the notes drawn out, sounding ominous and dreary as opposed to the upbeat dance song it was supposed to be. Roger turned to face the TV, his face contorted with a cocktail of fear and confusion. Then the words came. They weren't the words to the song. They were spoken words that sounded painfully forced between the notes of the distorted music. He paled when he realized the voice was saying his name, calling him through the song bellowing from his television. The voice was distant and distorted and there was a strange static that crackled through the song, but Roger still recognized Alice's small voice. He felt overwhelmed with fear. What if Kara did hear it? What if Alice told his sister of his guilt? He couldn't bear to lose Kara. That loss would be far worse than Lisa's.

Roger turned away from the television to find the remote, only to find Kara standing there, having returned without him noticing. Roger jumped with a start which made her crack up laughing.

He tried to play it off by smiling and hitting her in the arm. He noticed the music sounded normal once more. What was happening? Was it even real? A shiver danced along his spine like a pirouetting ballerina, and he rolled his shoulders, squirming against the feel of it.

"How about we take this party on the road?" he asked. "Go somewhere where we can really dance and get our drink on?"

Kara responded with a big smile. She licked her teeth. "That's what I'm talking about," she said excitedly, bounding out the door of his apartment.

Roger snatched up the remote and quickly shut off the TV. He made sure his sister wasn't looking in as he hurriedly cleaned the wet spot on the carpet before running out to meet her in the hall.

8

MAYBE MUSIC WAS NOT the best idea after all, Roger thought as he bit his lip against the memory. He eyed the crowd walking the opposite direction, on the other side of the street. This was something he always did. It kept his mind off other things and made him less aware of how many people were close to him on his side of the street. It was a way to prevent an anxiety trigger from happening. Whenever he felt crowded, he felt panicked. Maybe it stemmed from the day at the circus. He didn't know. He had plenty to bring up to Mark when he next saw him, but the man probably needed a break after the bomb Roger dropped on him today.

Roger looked at the people around, watched them walk in each of their signature fashions. It fascinated him how everyone had their own personal gait and no two people moved exactly the same. He listened to their odd conversations that reached him as they went by, trying to make sense out of them as he only caught random snippets. Sometimes it was a fun game to imagine what the rest of it could be. He was sure his imaginary version was much more exciting than the reality, but it was fun, nonetheless. It brought him a genuine smile for the first time that day and he could almost hear Kara's voice telling him to lighten up.

The feeling of ease didn't last long though. As he watched and listened to the other people out there with him, he was reminded Alice had been in the back of the taxi. She could be out there with him now, couldn't she? As his eyes combed the crowd for any sign of the dead girl's presence, he thought back to a few days ago when he had seen her in person. She hadn't been as frighteningly decayed as she had today. She had looked just like the Alice he remembered. Roger had been home in his apartment. Kara wasn't there this time, but he did have music playing through his television.

Roger hadn't wanted to play music since the incident with Kara, but the silence was maddening. It left him to the mercy of his own thoughts and with the relentless brutality of his never-ending anxiety that was impossible to withstand. So, he put on a different channel to avoid any connection he could.

Roger had had a bad day at the office. He was overtired from everything going on. Between his own guilt and Alice's visits, he wasn't getting any sleep and it showed. On top of screwing things up and accidentally deleting an important file when he fell asleep in front of his computer, his boss had commented on his disheveled appearance and told him to go home and rest. Then she added, "Take a shower and put on some clean clothes before you come back here."

"Screw you," Roger thought as he walked shamefully out of the office and the building. None of those people had any idea what he was dealing with, and he doubted they would fare any better if they were in his shoes.

Now he was home, sitting in the same dirty clothes, dark rings under his bloodshot eyes, listening to music he didn't even like in an attempt to get out of his own head. It wasn't working.

A knock sounded at the door, and Roger thought it was the

landlord looking for the rent he didn't have yet and was unlikely to have soon if he didn't get to work. He rubbed at his face with both hands and pulled on his bottom lip, stretching it.

When the knock came again, Roger decided to get up and check. He supposed it could be Kara, but he doubted it as he knew she was supposed to be at work as well. It certainly wasn't going to be Lisa. Those days were long gone. With a huff, Roger approached the door. He put his palms against it and leaned forward to peer through the peephole at the distorted visage of the hallway beyond.

At first, he couldn't see anyone out there, only the tiled floor of the hallway through the glass as he pressed his eye against it. The knock sounded again as Roger stared out at the empty hall-way. He felt the vibrations from lower down the door. Whoever was knocking was shorter than he could see through the peep-hole. He was looking over their head at the hallway behind them.

Roger felt suddenly nervous, his heart picking up speed. He didn't move. He kept his palms on the door, staring out with a single eye. Moments passed by like hours, bringing with them more anxiety as each second ticked away. When the knock hadn't sounded in some time and he had yet to see anyone in the hallway, Roger felt ready to give up and abandon his post.

That's when she stepped backward into his view. Alice stared up at him as if she could see him through the peephole. Her eyes were big and full of sadness, and she clutched that filthy old doll in her tiny hand.

Roger held his breath. He didn't know what to do. He was afraid to move, to breathe, to make a sound. What did she want? Was she there for his soul?

Tears rolled down the child's pale cheeks as she stared up at him. She obviously knew he was there, that he was watching her. Roger's fingers became claw-like, scraping against his side of the door. He felt so awful for her, so terrible for what he had done, but he was as afraid of her now as he was of her father the day it all happened. He hated himself for being such a coward.

"Face her," his inner voice commanded. "Be a man for once and face her."

Roger stepped back away from the door. He covered his face with his hands as he continued to face the door and the dead child he knew stood on the other side of it. Tears spilled out of his own eyes, rolling over the edge of his hands like river water washing over rocks.

"Face her, dammit."

The knock came again, and Roger trembled. He cried harder, hoping to stifle the sound of it with his tightly clamped hands.

"Face her."

Roger lashed out and seized the doorknob before he lost his nerve. He quickly turned it before any anxious thoughts could enter his mind and talk him out of it. Roger pulled the door open inward and found himself standing before an empty hallway.

Unable to hold himself up any longer, he sank to his knees. With his shaking hands, he touched his fingertips to the space where she had just stood. Behind him, the music coming from his television became skewed, slowing down, the notes warping. Roger clamped his dusty hands over his mouth again. He held them there as tightly as he could and screamed into his palms.

9

THERE WERE a multitude of different people today, Roger noticed as he took his mind off Alice to get back to people watching. Business types talked to unseen people on their wireless earbuds. Young children toted ice cream cones before the season became too cold to eat them. Teenagers, some in sweaters and some in full on Gothic attire, were more concerned with their fashion statement than the growing chill in the air. There were old people doing their best to make it around, and young people excitedly chugging along. Some were on bicycles like the delivery people in their work uniforms. Couples held hands, and friends laughed.

Then he spotted little black shoes and white stockings. He couldn't see the face of the girl wearing them, but it reminded him of Alice and the outfit she was now doomed to wear forever. He pictured her in his mind, remembering her staring at him from inside the taxi, and he felt his anxiety returning with a vengeance. He just needed to see the girl the shoes belonged to, and he would see it wasn't her and know his fear was just getting the best of him.

But what if it *was* her, stalking him out in the world, coming for him, for her revenge? If she had been in the taxi, it was possible, wasn't it? Roger did not want to take chances by sticking around. He wanted to bolt, but his legs wouldn't allow it. He banged his hand on the side of his head, trying to knock himself rational.

Maybe it was his mind playing tricks on him, his guilt manifesting itself in a frightening way and nothing more than that. He screamed at himself inside his mind until he finally listened. *You're going insane! Get a hold of yourself!*

Looking away from the crowd, he focused his gaze straight ahead and walked on. Unfortunately, this brought all the people walking around him into his focus and he felt suddenly confined, afraid, paranoid, and constricted. He tried singing a song to himself, focusing on the words, drumming the beat on his hip with his fingers. It wasn't working. He was fighting the urge to scream at the unsuspecting strangers to back away and give him space. He already felt like they were staring at him. It wasn't entirely untrue. Makeup lady had noticed him, hadn't she?

A gentle breeze blew past him as he walked, and he could swear it carried his name past his ears. It was faint, but clear as day and very much impossible. It gave more weight to his theory that his mind was at fault. It would also explain why the cab driver hadn't seen Alice in his backseat. He was losing it. He needed sleep. That was all it was. Roger had to get home and get some sleep. Would Alice let him?

After a brief hesitation, Roger started walking again, determined to remain sane.

"Roger?" a child's voice said, louder this time. He recognized the voice, but he tried not to pay attention to it. He didn't believe it was real. It couldn't be. She died at Sunnycrest. Her spirit should be at Sunnycrest. She shouldn't be here. Not like this.

Roger's eyes danced across the passing faces and no one else reacted as if they heard anything. That should be proof enough, shouldn't it?

Kara hadn't seemed to have heard Alice in the music that day either. He didn't know what to believe, but he knew what he wanted to believe. *It's in my head. It's in my head.*

"Roger."

No.

"Roger."

It's in my head.

"Roger."

The voice was followed by a familiar giggle this time, as the breeze came again, ruffling his clothes. It wasn't strange for there to be a breeze at the start of fall, but it didn't seem to be affecting the others on the street. Their clothing and books and briefcases all remained still. He stopped in his tracks and started panting again. Real or not, it scared him, the wind, and the voice it brought with it, the laughter trailing behind.

"Please," he mumbled quietly. "Please. I'm sorry."

Someone beside him heard him and paid him a wary sideways glance, which he frowned at. He was drawing attention to himself and that was the last thing he wanted to do.

Roger couldn't stop the anxiety now. At this rate, he was going to hyperventilate before the day was through. His sweating hands gripped at his shirt, curling the fabric over his fingertips as he closed his eyes and tried hard to regain control of himself.

"Roger. Roger, look," the voice said, sounding like it was spoken by several children, all dancing around him in a circle, creating their own breeze that chilled him to the bone. He felt like he was standing in the center of a game of *Ring Around the Rosie.*

Roger turned his head ever so slowly to glance back at the passing crowd across the street to look for the black shoes, to see what the children wanted him to see. Were they other children who had passed, who she brought with her from the other side to torment him?

As he turned to look, time seemed to slow until it almost halted entirely. Even the sounds of the city slowed, dropping in octaves, and dragging syllables like the music from his television. All of this was impossible, wasn't it?

The crowd moved in slow motion before his eyes, passing him by with a painstaking lethargy. As they went, he could see they were leaving one behind, one who was not moving at all: the owner of the black shoes and white stockings. Roger felt frozen. He could do nothing but stare, his eyes laser focused on the scene before him. He didn't want to see who the shoes belonged to, but he knew that he needed to, they needed him to.

He felt like his heart slowed to match the pace of the passersby, and it was eventually going to stop entirely. Part of him wished it would, that this would all finally be over, even if Alice was waiting for him in the afterlife, prepared to greet him with open arms.

More and more of the people moved by, each step a horrible eternity. As they went, more of the little girl who was hidden behind them became visible. He wished time would accelerate to a normal pace and he could just get it over with, but he knew this was her game and he would have to play by her rules. Her white stockings and the frill of her black dress became clear then. His hands felt suddenly arthritic and froze in a claw-like grip at his sides. What would happen once he saw her in full? Would she cross the street and come for him, come to take his life as he had taken hers? Would the other children hold him there until she could reach him? What would they do to him then?

Roger felt like his feet had been nailed to the pavement where he stood, like a hand had a grip on the back of his head, forcing it in her direction, pushing against him if he tried to turn. He fought against it and failed. Someone wanted him to see and wouldn't allow him to escape. Was it anxiety or was it truly the dead?

Roger started to see the little girl's dress in full. Her pale arms swung back and forth at her sides, faster than the movement of everyone around her, a filthy, naked doll clutched in her right hand, hair moving about with the rhythmic swinging of her arm. Roger knew that doll, the plastic head and fabric body, stitches popping and stained with years of play. He had seen that doll fall from Alice's dead fingers and land on the laundry room floor where he left it. Couldn't it have gone to Goodwill or Salvation Army where it was purchased by another child? He was still trying to rationalize, to fight against the truth. It could still be someone else. He was paranoid. Maybe another family had found the doll there in the laundry room and given it to their own daughter thinking she would enjoy it.

An elderly man pushing a walker moved past her and Roger spied her black hair blowing in the gentle breeze that only existed around her, just like the breeze around him earlier. As more and more people made their way past, trudging as if they were trying to swim through mud, more of her whipping hair came into view. Her pale neck was blue tinted with scrawling veins.

Roger's heart raced as if it was opposing the slowness of the situation, fighting back against it with anxiety. He wished they would just move and get it over with. He wanted to scream. He tried to. The same hand that held his head in place held his mouth shut, and it hurt as he strained to pry his teeth apart, like they had been glued together.

Let it happen! Show her. Let him see what he was meant to see so he could be done with it and move on, or die, or whatever was meant to happen. He just couldn't stand the wait anymore. It felt like torture. Maybe it was. Maybe this was her revenge. She was intent on making him suffer. Whatever the outcome, Roger knew one thing for sure; this was a game. Even in death, Alice was a child, and she was playing with him. She wanted it to last, to nag at him, to make him crazy. It was going to take forever because she knew he wanted it to be over with and she would never let him have what he wanted, not after what he did to her. That's exactly what this was, and he knew it. She needed to display she was the one in control.

I'm sorry! He screamed within the confines of his head, since his mouth couldn't move to actually voice the words. Tears formed in his eyes and gently rolled down his frozen face. He found he couldn't even blink, like his eyes had been taped open. *Please!*

The voices of the passing crowd had slowed down to match the speed of their lethargic movements. The inevitable was so close to finally being revealed to him as the last few stragglers made their way past. He clawed at his shirt with the stiff, rigid fingers of his gnarled hands as he watched for her to finally come into view, at last. Roger started to hold his breath.

In an instant, the last people passed by, and time went back to normal, resuming its usual pace. No one was there. She was gone completely. There were no black shoes, no black hair, no black dress or white stockings, no pale skin, nothing. She was just *gone* as if she had never been there at all. With her disappearance, his movement returned to him, unrestricted. The invisible hands that held him pulled away.

It didn't make sense after all that time, all that waiting. Why? Was it just to make him crazy? Did she mean to drive him mad?

Roger massaged his jaw and opened and closed his mouth, his teeth and bones still aching from the force of the clutching hands. He had a headache now, thrumming at his temple. His stomach felt sick. He spun in a circle looking every which way for any sign that a child had really been there, that what he had seen had been real. What he found were tons of faces of all ages and colors, staring at him with judgment, as if they knew he was haunted and brought something evil to the street where they walked.

He could hear giggles coming from every which way, but he could see no children at all on the street, aside from one boy who stared at him like the rest as he passed by holding his mother's hand.

A shiver crawled like a scurrying rodent up his back, its tiny feet dancing over his spine. He walked in a circle, looking every which way, searching for a sign, a small detail of what he knew had to be there. He knew she wouldn't go through all that trouble just to leave him there alone. She was still watching him from somewhere. She had to be.

No. She didn't, did she? Not if she were just a trick of his guilt-ridden, addled mind. He was losing it. He had heard stories of grief manifesting in similar ways. He just needed to get home, to get off these streets and be safe behind a locked door. He almost laughed at the thought. Locked doors didn't keep ghosts out. It was all an illusion he chose to believe in. Home was a placebo, one people used to convince themselves they were safe. But was there ever safety from a spirit haunting you? Was there safety from your own mind? Now that he had seen her out here in the world, Roger didn't think anywhere was safe.

Illusion or not, home was all he had aside from his sister who was busy at work. He thought of how many times home had been his respite from Alice's father and his anger, good intentions or not. He thought of one time in particular.

Roger had gone grocery shopping at the corner store. Since he walked and had to carry things up to the seventh floor, he usually didn't buy a lot at a time. This day had been an exception since it was date night. Lisa was coming over and he was cooking dinner, so he decided to go all out. He was making a German meatloaf with a Stroganoff mushroom gravy, a side of homemade mashed potatoes with garlic and chives, and, of course, the accompanying corn and sauteed vegetables. He'd picked up a nice bottle of wine to go with dinner as well, and the ingredients to bake her a German chocolate cake for dessert to stay with the theme. Lisa loved coconut so it should have been a good choice.

When Roger got back to Sunnycrest hugging paper bags of

groceries in both arms, the maintenance man, Tom, was hanging an *Out of Order* sign on the tied-off stairwell door.

"Something wrong?" Roger asked him. He didn't use the stairs much. They were old and not in good shape and they wound back and forth with a space to fall in between them. It messed with his anxiety. Still, it felt worrisome to see them taped off. He couldn't help but wonder if somebody had fallen.

Tom looked at him, his eyes quivering, and his face pulled toward the ground by the weight of a sadness Roger didn't understand. "Certain time of year, the stairs just ain't no good."

Roger watched the man walking away and thought the answer had been a bit strange. The entire encounter was odd. He would have shrugged had it not been for the arms full of groceries. As it was, he couldn't even push the button for the elevator. He had to lift his legs and hit it with his foot and when he did, he struggled to not drop the bags in his arms, yelping as they slipped, but he caught and adjusted them.

When the doors opened, Roger shifted for a better grip on the groceries then slipped into the box. The doors started to slide closed when a large, calloused hand stopped them. Roger watched with wary eyes as the doors were pried open. Alice's father, Brian pushed his way into the elevator. He was quaking with adrenaline, his face red with the boiling anger in his veins. He shot Roger a look as if to say, *what are you staring at?*

Roger swallowed the lump that rose in his throat. He turned his eyes forward and watched the number, but his heart raced, and he had to shift the bags more to adjust for the sweating of his palms. There was a violent *BANG* as Brian drove a fist into the wall of the elevator. The loud, sudden noise made Roger twitch and the bags started to slip.

When they reached their floor and the doors opened, Roger moved to run out and get away from the danger of his neighbor's harbored anger. He slipped and the groceries fell from his arms. He slid across the tiled floor holding empty paper bags in a cascade of ingredients that bounced and rolled all over the hall.

"What the hell is wrong with you?" Brian asked as he stepped over Roger to go into his own apartment and slam the door.

Roger cringed and covered his head as the man's shadow swept over him. With a yelp, Roger scrambled to his feet and ran to his own door. He fumbled with his key until he got it open, and it wasn't until he was inside against the closed door that he felt safe. He was still panting and trembling when there was a knock.

Could it be him?

Roger slid slowly up the door as the knock repeated. He squinted one eye while tightly shutting the other to peer through the tiny peephole and inspect the hallway for danger. He sighed with relief as his muscles unclenched and his shoulders relaxed. He straightened and opened the door.

Lisa was standing before him. She gestured to the mess in the hall. "Was all this our dinner?"

Roger frowned. "I'll give you a rain check on the home cooking," he told her. "Let's go out, my treat."

Lisa studied him for a moment as he came out and locked up. "You gonna tell me what happened here?"

"I'd rather hear about your day. I'm sure it's more interesting," Roger answered as he led her to the elevator.

When he pushed the button, he glanced over at Apartment 33 and a pang of fear seized him, but he did his best not to let it show. He anticipated the door flying open and the angry man raging through it. Roger knew the man's anger wasn't directed at him, but he couldn't handle that level of anger at all, just being in the presence of it. There was a reason his father wasn't around when he and Kara were growing up, but the imprint of his anger remained.

10

AFTER FINDING no sign of the girl that had been either a ghost or a trick of the eye on the street, Roger started on his way again. Now, he walked with an edge of paranoia. He was constantly looking over his shoulder and scanning his surroundings from top to bottom, his eyes moving left and right, flitting around like gnats. It was very much the way he had lived when Brian was across the hall. His fury had been terrifying. If it frightened Roger the way it had, how had it been for Alice? Could his anger have been the reason Alice's mother had never been in the picture? It made sense to Roger, but why would she leave her child with such a monster?

Roger didn't know the truth and he didn't know if he ever would, but he knew how Alice saw it. As scared as she was of her father, she saw Roger as the bad guy. She had to, or she wouldn't aim to punish him like she did. She wouldn't follow, harass, and torment him. Was her father getting a taste of the same thing in his cell? Roger wasn't about to visit him and find out. He did that once already and it didn't go well.

Roger thought about the last time he saw Alice before she showed up in the taxi today, the first time he realized she wasn't an innocent child anymore, that she was something darker and more sinister. This Alice—the dark Alice—was something he had created. She was a curse born out of his lies. At least that's what his *I saw too many horror movies* mind conjured up as an answer to it all. She had been a sweet, vibrant kid and so full of life and energy, but she came back as something different.

Roger headed down to check the mail when a ball came rolling toward him, resting at his foot. It was one of those big plastic balls you get at the grocery store that looked like it had been tie-dyed, blazing with swirls of color.

Roger had seen this exact ball before, and he swallowed nervously at the sight of it. Alice used to run around outside kicking this very ball around the front yard of the apartment complex. Sometimes, she would kick it down their hall. She had almost tripped him with it on several occasions which earned her a scolding from her father. It made Roger flinch. He didn't ever want to be the reason she got screamed at and punished.

He almost said, "Don't defend me. She's fine," but he was too afraid of the man to utter any actual sound.

Not wanting to think about the ball now or the possibilities of where it came from, Roger moved the ball to the side with the toe of his shoe. He walked past it and heard a giggle behind him. He closed his eyes and took a deep breath, then kept walking.

Something hit him in the back, and he knew from the sound of it bouncing along the tiles that it was the ball, that ball... thrown by the unseen... Roger shook his head and told himself he was crazy. *It can't be Alice. It's very possible for another child to have the same ball. Some kid is messing with you.*

He stopped at the elevator and hit the button.

Roger did his best not to think about Alice as he waited for the doors to open. He tried to think about what he was going to have for dinner. He decided on BLATs because adding avocado to a BLT made it something far superior for some reason, and the thought made him smile.

The doors slid open, and Alice stood in the elevator. She had her head down and her hair draped in front of her face, but he knew it was her. She was wearing a black dress and little black shoes with buckles. She was bouncing the ball and catching it with both hands in a loud, steady rhythm.

Boom.

Boom.

Boom.

Boom.

Roger closed his eyes and shook his head and told himself it wasn't real.

"Open your eyes," her voice called to him from the elevator.

Roger told himself not to listen. He felt something take his hand, tugging it back toward his apartment. She couldn't be in two places at once, could she? Was it somebody else, another ghost, a person that knew he needed help? Roger had to know, and the only way to know was to open his eyes. He took a slow deep breath and did just that.

He didn't see anyone there, but he still felt the tug on his hand. He could hear the ball bouncing on the metal floor of the open elevator. Roger turned his head to look that way and found Alice right at the edge of the open doors. She was staring up at him with eyes burning with the fire of hate. Her hand lashed out and elongated black nails swiped at him like an animal's claws. Roger screamed and fell backward to avoid the attack.

Alice continued to stare at him, while someone or something else continued to tug at his hand. They were trying so hard to drag him away. Roger was too afraid to scream. *What was happening?*

It was all so insane, so terrifyingly insane that Roger just wanted to give up and cry. Alice leaned forward from the elevator. Her mouth opened and her bottom jaw lowered so far it almost rested on the floor at her feet. As Roger watched in horror, the dead child screamed. It wasn't a human scream, not the scream he had heard so many times from her in the days when she had been alive. It was high-pitched, other worldly, ethereal, and painful.

She moved to step toward him and her leg broke, snapping at the hip and turning awkwardly. She stepped forward anyway, dragging the broken limb behind her. Whoever pulled on Roger's hand won out, and he was dragged across the tiles toward his apartment. He screamed as he was pulled along, despite the fact he felt deep down whoever had his hand was rescuing him from the child he had killed and her vengeance.

"What in the hell is all the yelling about?"

Roger looked up and saw one of his neighbors. He frowned. How could he possibly explain to her what was going on? Her name was Tina. Tina Weathers. She ran a fruit stand downtown with her grandpa.

Roger noticed that his hand felt lighter, free once more. He looked down the hall toward the elevator and Alice was also gone as far as he could tell. Feeling embarrassed, he stood and brushed the dust off his clothes.

"What were you doing on the floor?" Tina inquired.

"Long story," Roger told her.

"Well, from now on, I hope your long stories don't require so much screaming."

"Yeah, about that," he said. "Do you believe in ghosts?"

"Of course I do," she answered. "I live at Sunnycrest." Then she backed into her apartment and slammed the door.

Roger sighed and looked at her door. Number 31. He bit his lip. His hand raised to knock but hovered there. He wanted her to elaborate, to tell him what she meant by that, but then he thought, *do I really?*

Sighing, he lowered his hand and went home. In the distance, he could hear a bouncing ball.

Boom.
Boom.
Boom.
Boom.

11

ROGER SPOTTED the entrance for the subway and decided it was probably his best bet. It was the fastest way home, the fastest way off these crowded streets. Walking no longer seemed like a viable option. He was not safe from her out here anymore than he was if he had sat beside her in the back of the taxi. He wasn't truly safe from her anywhere, he now realized, the memory of her screaming, unhinged jaw still fresh in his mind. Knowing the threat was the same no matter where he was, Roger figured he might as well try to get home as fast as he possibly could. Home was at least home, and he could cry and talk back to her away from prying ears and eyes.

"I swear I'm not crazy!" He imagined himself turning in a circle, calling out to the strangers on the crowded city street.

Maybe it wasn't too late to beg Alice for forgiveness. If nothing else, he could at least die alone in his own bed and not out here in public as a humiliating spectacle for the city dwellers to view on their lunch breaks, a body to step over like the discarded homeless they never bothered with. His mind pictured the chipped yellow paint of the two-story suburban house he grew up in.

Taking a deep breath, Roger pulled a dollar from his wallet and handed it to a filthy man at his feet. Nicotine-stained fingers received it, but the raccoon-like eyes surrounded by dirt still pleaded. Roger sighed and reached in his wallet for a five. He placed it in the same outstretched fingers and then said, "That's all I've got."

It wasn't true as he had more cash on him, but it was true in the sense that it was all that he was able to spend. As it was, he wasn't going to make rent. He couldn't help but wonder if he would get evicted from Sunnycrest or fed to the furnace in the basement. None of his neighbors seemed afraid of the building, though many of them had acknowledged it was haunted. Maybe their experiences were with more friendly ghosts. He laughed to himself as he imagined Casper roaming around the Sunnycrest Apartments happily talking to everyone. He sighed with relief as he realized he could still laugh. *I'm not dead yet.*

Roger headed toward the stone stairwell. It smelled of urine, but he ignored it. That was part of the city, a souvenir of its chaos. Everything smelled like urine, but he rarely ever saw anyone producing it. Maybe it was ghost urine. The city was obviously haunted, Roger contended.

Getting to the entrance in a hurry, Roger slowed down and walked with hesitation down the chipped and stained steps into the dimly lit subway station. It was one of the only places that stayed dark and gloomy even during the light of day. It was not even six o'clock in the evening, and he felt like he was descending into the depths of Hell.

Swallowing hard, Roger walked nervously, as he thought back to when he first moved into the Sunnycrest Apartment building. Kara was already established in the city when he moved here. He had stayed with her as he looked for a place of his own. Kara didn't mind having him, but her cat definitely did, and Roger needed his own space anyway.

Roger stood beside his sister, biting his lip, and staring at the terrible couch in the furnished apartment on the seventh floor of the thirteen-floor building. "I don't know," he said.

Kara laughed and rolled her eyes. "This place is a steal, Rodge. Plus, you can always get a new couch."

Roger frowned. "Onto the seventh floor? That sounds like a huge hassle. I think it would be less painful to keep it. It really is hideous though. Is that plaid? Who has a plaid couch this day and age?"

Kara laughed. "Apparently, you do. Come on. Sign the paper. You'd be silly not to take it. It's just a few stops away from me. It's not far from your job. There's great restaurants and that kick-ass bookstore down the block. You've got a park in walking distance. It's perfect."

"It's the city," Roger huffed. "Everything is in walking distance."

"What about a couch cover? That's easy."

Roger thought seriously about the suggestion. It wasn't a bad idea. He looked at the small, old woman standing in the kitchen doorway waiting on his decision. "The person that lived here.... why didn't they take any of their stuff?"

"Didn't need it," the woman said matter-of-factly.

Roger bit his lip and thought some more. Kara tapped his arm and met his eyes with a pleading look when he turned her way.

He sighed. "Alright. I'll take it," he said.

The woman was all business. She got him to fill out the paperwork, took his first and last month's rent, and wrote him a receipt for it. Then she handed him the keys and left him there.

"I like her," Kara said as she walked away.

Later that day, when Roger returned without his sister and a taxi full of his things, a lanky man with sagging skin under his chestnut eyes offered him assistance getting everything inside. "Thanks. I really appreciate it," Roger told the man.

"No problem at all. I'm Rasmus. I live on floor three. You taking the place on floor seven?"

"That's the one," Roger said, groaning as he dragged his stuff up into the old building.

"Sad Mary passed like she did, but I'm glad she got to reconnect with her husband."

"Mary?" Roger asked as he waited before the elevator.

"The woman who lived there before you. Dropped dead about a week ago, but it's alright. I saw her and her husband on Thursday. They seem well."

As Roger squeezed past all of his things into the elevator with an *oomph*, he thought about what Rasmus had just said. "Wait. You saw her after she died?"

The tall man smiled showing a single dimple on his right cheek. "It takes some getting used to, but you'll figure it out after a while," he said.

Roger had no idea what the man was talking about, but he was starting to regret accepting the guy's help. It was good to learn the neighbors though, who to talk to and who not to.

"Thanks for all your help," Roger said when they got to his door. "I'll take it from here. I'm pretty particular about where and how I want things." *Translation: I have crippling anxiety.*

Rasmus studied him for a moment. Then he nodded. "I'll see you around."

"Hopefully not like you saw Mary," Roger said with a nervous laugh.

Rasmus just shrugged and headed back to the elevator.

"Awesome," Roger said when he left. He used his new key to open his door and lugged some of his things inside. "I hope you've actually moved out of here, Mary," he said out loud to the empty, quiet apartment. "Um, and your husband, but uh, no hard feelings. I uh, wish you the best. Sorry."

12

AS DRAB AND dreary as the subway was, it was still the fastest means of travel available to him. When he reached the bottom of the steps, Roger found himself feeling a little better. Relief came with the large crowd talking amongst themselves. He didn't want to be in a crowd and surrounded by so many people, but there was safety in numbers, right? Now he was going to be part of the crowd for a change, instead of alone on the other side of the street watching the crowd go by. He still felt suffocated and anxious by their close proximity, but he told himself he was safer with them. His anxiety didn't seem to believe him though and provided clammy sweat and labored breathing anyway.

Roger couldn't help but wonder what would happen if they were like the taxi driver and unable to see Alice if she showed up. That would be miserable. He would be stuck in a mob of people and unable to avoid her. Maybe the crowd wasn't a benefit after all. He quickly pushed the thought out of his mind before it spiraled out of control and sent his anxiety on a rampage. Anxiety had a way of making everything seem like the wrong answer. That was what it did. He couldn't listen to it. Unfortunately, it didn't listen to him either and resented being told to hush.

Roger stopped when he reached the mass of people waiting on the train to arrive. He took a deep breath before digging in his pocket for a token. He didn't keep a metro card because he didn't go out enough. When he did get tokens, he got several, so he wouldn't have to deal with the subway clerks for a while. They weren't always friendly. Plus, Kara and Mark were pretty much the only living humans he talked to anymore since Lisa left him. He conversed with his boss Elena, and coworkers when he had to, but he kept it to work related matters.

A rapid thumping sound drew Roger's attention back to the steps. He watched as a child's ball bounced down slowly and stopped at his feet. His breath immediately caught in his chest. Slowly, he tilted his head down and looked at the large plastic ball. It was white and covered in swirls of color like food dye dripped into a bowl of milk.

Could it be hers? Was this another game? Was Alice toying with him some more? He pictured her in his mind kicking the ball around the front yard and stopping to look up at him as he walked by into the building with a gleeful smile on her face. It drove a dagger of guilt into his heart.

Still, the sight of the ball at his feet frightened him. Even as it stood still before him, as if the toy itself was urging him to pick it up, he could still hear the slow thumping it made as it hit each step on its way down.

Boom.

Boom.

Boom.

Boom.

Pick me up! Get me, so you can play with her. She's waiting for you. Come on, Roger.

Roger shook his head. He was really going out of his mind. He could hear the voice of a child calling to him. It didn't call him by name like the voice carried on the wind when he was on the street, but he knew—without hearing the words—the voice was meant for him. Somehow, he could feel it. Just like the ball, the owner beckoned him, trying to drag him into their game.

Even slower than he looked down at the ball, Roger raised his gaze to peer up the stone subway steps, anxious to see if it was

Alice waiting for him at the top of the landing. He moved under the weight of panic, raising his head what seemed to be no more than an inch a minute, his hands trembling as his bones shook within him.

The voice was getting louder by the second which only heightened his fear. It was flooding his ears. The child was angry, demanding. They were going to hold him again, not let him go, like the phantom children that made him watch on the street or the hand that tugged him toward his apartment that day. Was this to be how things were now? Punishment after punishment, cruel game after game, she was going to torment him until she broke him entirely. He wished it would end, that she would fly down the steps and plunge those black talons into his beating heart to still it for good.

Roger didn't want to die. His guilt wanted him to die. He wanted to run, to escape and live on, though he wasn't sure what for. It was instinct, ingrained, a need to survive, but the truth was there was nowhere to go unless he wanted to jump onto the tracks and make his way into the deeper darkness of the adjoining tunnel and whatever would be waiting for him there. That was if the tons of people gathered all around wouldn't grab him and stop him from even making that jump. Then if they had him held up, his arms or legs restricted, he would be left at Alice's mercy and chances were the people confining him wouldn't see her or realize the true weight of the threat upon him. Would they see him die in their arms once she made it to him? He could imagine their screams, if they witnessed his death but couldn't see the person committing the heinous act. *That ought to bring Mark more business*, he thought cynically.

The voice sounded so angry, furious, but his mind seemed to be blocking the words from reaching his ears. He knew a child commanded him. It sounded similar to Alice's voice, but also different. Maybe it was distorted from crossing the plane into the realm of the living, but it hadn't been distorted before. Why would it be different this time? He had too many questions.

When his eyes finally found their way to the top of the steps, they came to rest upon two small children: a girl and a boy standing together. They were screaming at him. It was as if someone had hit the mute button on a remote to a TV that had been on full volume, and now just unmuted it, returning the world to its blasting entirety. When the jarring sound returned, it caused him to jump.

"Hey, Mister! What's wrong with you? Throw the ball! Can you hear me? Are you deaf or just crazy? Just throw us the ball!"

Roger couldn't help but laugh, which probably didn't help his case against being crazy. He was not sure if the situation was actually humorous or if madness really was setting in. Whether it was funny or not, people were sure to think he was out of his mind if he continued to go on like this. The children at the top of the stairs obviously already did. They plainly said so. He waved a friendly hand at them.

"Sorry! I was lost in thought."

Bending down, he picked their ball up and gave it a good toss toward the top of the stairs. It hit a step, two from the top and bounced. The little boy reached out quickly and grabbed it with two hands, a scowl on his face.

"Thank you!" he yelled down the steps, his voice riddled with disdain.

"Sorry again," Roger called back. He laughed at himself and watched with a smile as the children ran off into the safety of daylight. His smile faded quickly though as he watched Alice running with them, lagging slightly behind. She looked like her usual self, her old self, not the evil, rotted version of her that had been appearing to him today. She turned her head and smiled, her knowing eyes meeting his, as she followed the other children out of sight, giggling happily as she skipped away.

The way she seemed to play with the unknowing children was far from threatening but it still frightened Roger. Seeing her at all scared him at this point. Still, appearing as her healthy self hit him in the heart as well. He thought of the one time he saw her truly happy when she was still alive, before he had interfered in her life and helped her to her death. She was so vibrant, a little girl with a big personality.

Roger was sitting outside under the big tree, the one place of shade Sunnycrest had to offer against the blazing sun. He had a notepad and a pen that was fancier than he had the right to carry. It was a gift from the boss at his new job. Elena Maxwell said no businessman wrote with dime store pens. She told him clients believed in what they saw and they would always compare him to the businessmen from television and books. Roger had nodded and thanked her.

Now he used said pen to try to write a letter to Lisa. He wanted her to understand he loved her and was serious about their relationship. He also wanted to explain that he suffered from PTSD due to childhood trauma that had led to a severe anxiety disorder, depression, and a complete aversion to yelling. He wanted to make her understand his less than favorable reaction to Brian and Alice. Unfortunately, everything he wrote sounded like he was completely crazy when he read it back. He wanted her to forgive him, not give her more reasons to stay away. *Oh okay, you were scared because you're insane. I'll be right over.*

Roger had never been much of a writer. Anytime school required essays he struggled. Somehow, he still managed to make it to an associate degree. With his charming smile and friendly demeanor, sales came naturally, regardless of his choice of pens. Yet, he still couldn't figure out how to sell himself to his own girlfriend.

There was a creak as the ancient front door came open, and it drew Roger's gaze. Alice came flying out of the building, bouncing down the stairs with a skip in her step. She squealed loudly and spun in a circle with her arms out at her sides, her dress fanning out around her. Roger found himself smiling, feeling her excitement. He had never seen her like this. It was impossible for her happiness not to be contagious.

"Hi!" she shouted gleefully, waving at him. Her other hand clutched that filthy doll she loved so much. She held it up before her and acted like she was dancing with the woman. Roger suppressed a laugh.

He found himself jotting ideas down on his paper. He was trying to guess what could have made her so happy. A puppy? Some other new pet? Her mother coming home?

"I have a boyfriend," she said to him, giving him the answer before he asked.

Roger raised his eyebrows. "Oh yeah?"

"Yup. I met him at school. His name is Peter. His dad is a mailman, and his mother is a dancer and he's super nice and he likes Lady Gaga too and he has blond hair, but his mom doesn't. She has brown hair and she's really pretty and her car is nicer than my dad's but it's okay because there's more to life than money."

Roger nodded and laughed, eyes wide. "Absolutely. You are very wise," he told her.

A sudden bang made him jump and drop his pen. He watched it roll away down the sloped walkway and into the street where it fell into a sewer grate. He sighed, his shoulders slumping. When he looked back, he saw Alice's father dragging her by the wrist back into the building. Roger's heart sank at the sight of the girl's missing smile and exuberance she had just shown.

"I hate you!" she screamed at her father as the door fell shut.

Roger sighed. He stood up and brushed himself off. With no pen, the pad was useless. It wasn't getting him anywhere anyway. He would just buy her a comic book and some flowers and hope that was enough to explain his feelings.

He exhaled his frustration and sudden sadness and walked to the trash can beside the building. Roger threw the pad inside the waste basket, then pulled the big door open, cringing at its squeal. He craned his neck to make sure Brian and Alice were gone before he headed inside and hit the *up* button on the elevator.

When the elevator doors opened, a man stepped out and grabbed Roger's shoulders, staring into his eyes. "Have you seen my wife? My name is Stanley. I live on floor nine. I can't find my wife. I think my Kathy is hurt."

Roger just shook his head. "N-no. I'm sorry. I haven't seen her."

The man ran past Roger toward the door to the stairwell. Roger, feeling even more uncomfortable than he already was, stepped into the elevator and hit the button for floor seven.

13

CONVINCED NOW that he was surely losing his sanity, Roger dug deep into his pocket until he managed to fish out his token. With shaking hands, he pushed it into the turn-style and crossed through to the other side where the pile of people laid waiting, unaware of him or the spirit that haunted him.

He couldn't help looking over his shoulder to make sure she was really gone. He had seen her follow those other children, but he didn't believe anything he saw anymore nor anything he heard or felt. A few people glanced his way but none for long. There were always strange types at the subway, so it stopped fazing people after a while. He probably seemed normal down here. Maybe he *was* normal. Maybe the whole city was haunted? How was he to know?

Trying to stay calm and remain inconspicuous, Roger strolled over to join the crowd waiting for the next train to arrive. The man next to him looked up from his paper to glance at Roger and then quickly returned his gaze to the newsprint. Roger swallowed hard and focused on the train tracks, his foot tapping nervously. He wished he had a paper of his own, something to read and focus on to take his mind off all that had happened today. He didn't want to think about all the memories that kept popping into his anxious mind. He didn't want to think about any of it.

He should have bought a paper at the kiosk but he didn't want to work his way through the crowd to go back. Just looking at them all made him sweat. There were more than there had been when he had entered. So many.

God forbid there was a fire down here. We would all die, he thought.

He would remember this and make sure to get a paper next time should he gather the courage to leave the house again. At this moment, it didn't seem likely.

A rumbling came from the dark tunnel to the left. Roger sighed with relief. He was glad he wasn't going to have to wait long. His collar was tightening, strangling him. He wondered if people noticed, if their eyes rose above their papers to analyze him. He didn't know, wouldn't know, because he couldn't bear to look at them. Let them judge him if they wanted to. It didn't matter. None of it mattered anymore.

The rumbling proved to be a train, as he thought, but it was moving way too fast to be his train which made him frown and feel discouraged. It must be an express train just passing through. Onlookers clutched their papers more tightly, prepared for the breeze the speeding behemoth would generate.

As it chugged by, Roger saw Alice's pale face glaring at him through a window in the first car. It went by quickly, but he knew what he saw. She was dead again, long dead. It wasn't the Alice that ran after the kids on the street, the Alice from his memory. This was the Alice from the taxi. He shivered and rolled his shoulders to try to remain composed.

Taking a deep breath, Roger tried his best to act like a typical city goer and pretend he didn't see the dead girl. *Just let it pass,* he told himself. *Practice indifference, apathy, the American way. Don't give her power. You can do this. Just let her go. The train will be gone in a moment. Everything is going to be fine.*

The act became harder to deliver convincingly when he saw her again at the window of the next car, small, pale palms against the dirty glass, staring out at him with those hate-filled, green eyes that almost glowed in the darkness of the subway. What was the point? What did she want?

Though her head was fixed straight ahead, her eyes seemed to follow him, finding him even as she passed by like the legendary stare of the painted Mona Lisa. As soon as she zipped by out of sight, she was at the next window, and the next after that, staring at him from every passing car. It was impossible but somehow made perfect sense.

"No," Roger mumbled quietly, his sweating hands nervously fidgeting before him. "No, no, no." Internally, he screamed for her to go away.

As the train roared by, Roger found Alice at every passing window, her tiny ghostly hands scaling the glass, gripping and scratching at it, the mottled black and blue veins spreading up her neck and over her face, growing further, like reaching branches of a dead tree climbing her face more each time he saw her, the infection of her death spreading before his eyes. She wanted him to see, to feel what he had done. To watch her rot and dissolve before his very eyes. *You did this!*

Roger squeezed his eyes shut tight so he wouldn't have to see her, but the image of her staring through the glass at him remained plastered behind his eyes. Even without his eyes open, he could see her as his ears listened to the passing rumble of the speeding train. Her head tipped back, and her mouth opened like a black void and a swarm of insects flew from her throat, buzzing toward him, surrounding him, engulfing him.

Roger squeezed his eyes shut even more tightly, trying to force the image from his mind. *It's not real. It's not real. It's not real.*

He listened as the train cars rumbled by one at a time. With his eyes closed painfully tight, he could still feel her stare like the heat of the sun, penetrating, burning into him. It was somehow painful, *physically* painful. He didn't need to see her to know she was there. His screams for her to go away almost made it to his mouth, but he thought of all the people standing around him and bit it back. The scream lodged in his throat like a tangible object, cutting off his air, needing to be dislodged.

When Roger finally opened his eyes, gasping, the last car of the speeding express train rumbled away into the tunnel to his right. Alice stood on the back end, bone white fingers clutching tightly to the railing. Her yarn-like, black hair whipped around in the breeze like Medusa's snakes, and her black dress ruffled like a flag. Her emerald eyes seemed to be missing now, replaced by nothing but two cavernous holes in her young face.

Even without eyes, the empty sockets filled only with the infinite darkness of death seemed to locate Roger in the crowd. Her mouth fell open and what looked like hundreds of worms poured from the opening, rolling over her blue-tinged, dead lips to fall to the tracks below, squirming as they went. Then she disappeared into the darkness of the tunnel.

Roger knew she wasn't going to stop unless he found a way to stop her. He needed to face her, to talk to her and find out what she wanted from him. He wasn't going to have that conversation here. He needed to get home, and when he did, he was finally going to stop running. Unfortunately, Roger knew all about running.

Roger was Alice's age, standing in a tiled kitchen covered in peeling, tacky, yellow wallpaper. His father knocked back the vodka, and Roger watched him with anticipation. For such a young child, he was well aware what happened when his dad took to the bottle.

His father didn't even live there. His mother had already thrown the man out for his drinking and the behavior it led to, but he still came around. He claimed he wanted to see his kids or sometimes just blatantly needed money. Roger's mother cursed him once he was gone, but she placated him while he was there. She gave him what he wanted, even if it was herself, just to get him on his way so they could get back to life.

Roger hated his father, but he wasn't as vocal about it as Kara. She would tell their father she hated him, yell it in his face before running into a different room and slamming the door. Their dad's reaction wasn't any more mature. He would slam the door back open, scream even louder, and break something Kara loved to punish her for disrespecting him. Eventually, their mom would intervene, do something to calm him, and distract him from the children until he could sleep it off.

Roger always watched, a fly on the wall, silent. He sat against the peeling yellow wall, hugging his knees to his chest, peering over the tops of them at his father. The man's voice was already getting louder.

Kara appeared in the doorway. "Just get out!" she screamed. "You don't live here! No one wants you here!"

Roger jumped when the glass shattered. It scattered over the floor, and his dad was already opening a new bottle as he marched toward Kara.

"I'm not afraid of you!" she yelled at him. "You're just a drunk!"

Roger's eyes widened as he watched the heavy hand come across his sister's face.

"Mom!" Kara screamed as she held her swelling cheek.

Roger was up and moving then. He ran past them all out the back door. He crossed the yard but didn't stop. He threw the gate open and kept running. He pumped his arms and churned his legs as he bolted into the woods and through the trees. He wanted to get as far away as he could, to be where his actual life couldn't be seen or heard, where he could pretend it didn't exist.

As he ran, he imagined a different reality, one where he lived among the animals of the forest and there was peace. Kara would come find him eventually. She always did. She would find him, and she would bring him back to that terrible house. He always felt so mad at her when she did that, but she was the strong one. He had to follow her, to trust her. He didn't want to think about any of that right now though. Right now, he just wanted to run.

14

ROGER CAME BACK from the trauma of his childhood into the trauma of his present. He stumbled backward, tripping over somebody's foot.

"Watch it," the man snapped at him.

Roger paid him no attention. He didn't even bother to offer up an apology. It was so inconsequential in the grand scheme of things. He realized he was haunted long before he ever met Alice. Roger imagined Hell would be his father on one side and Alice on the other. They were both dead. When Brian died, he could join the party.

Roger wanted to run like he did as a child. He wanted to flee, up the stairs and back to the street, but he knew Alice would come to get him like Kara used to. Running never got you anywhere. He needed to face his ghosts, even if it killed him.

Roger searched the area. He needed something to focus upon until his breathing and heart rate become regular again, something to help with the anxiety. At the current rate of his frightened heart, he felt like he would be joining Alice and his father in the afterlife before long. He needed to calm down. He had always wished he had his sister's strength, but he didn't and never would. This was who he was; an anxious frightened child. At least with Mark's help, he was able to control it.

As he searched frantically for something to distract him, Roger was making his situation worse. He was panicking, and his heart rate sped up rather than decelerated. His breathing bordered on hyperventilation, and everyone definitely was staring at him now. His eyes found their disgusted faces as he searched for something to take away his anxiety. The image of Alice's empty sockets returned to his mind, and he felt like crying. He wished he could breathe.

Roger wanted to yell at the other people waiting on the train, to scream at their staring faces and tell them they should mind their own business, but he couldn't find the breath to do it. In this particular instance, that was probably for the best.

Then he spotted it.

It was just what he needed.

There was a flashing red bulb on the side of the wall. He hadn't the faintest idea as to its purpose, but he knew what its purpose was going to be for him. Roger stared at the bulb intensely, tuning out the rest of the world to watch it blink.

On.

Off.

On.

Off.

Soon there was nothing else but the blinking bulb. The rest of the world just melted away. It was like he was standing in empty space, surrounded by pitch black darkness, the only other thing was the red bulb before him, flashing in the darkness, like a camera snapping photos. On. Off. Nothing else existed. He was safe here in the dark with this red light of his. It was a beacon of solace, guiding him back to health.

Slowly, his breathing became more regular. The beating of his heart calmed itself to a normal rhythm. Roger smiled, relieved. Mark knew his stuff. Roger thought of the day Mark had taught him this skill.

Roger had had a particularly bad day at work. He had been excited because he had several leads, but none of them bit and all the work he had done acquiring them had been for nothing. Now, his rent was due, he had no commission, and Elena Maxwell made sure he knew it.

He made it back to Sunnycrest where Brian was screaming per usual. It took him back to his own childhood, and he started to freak out. He went to leave the building and the land lady, Agatha, was at the door coming in to collect. Roger fled to the laundry room. He called Lisa who was still mad at him for the failed date the last time she had come over.

"Why are you calling me, Roger?"

Roger hung up. He felt completely alone, scared, and unable to breathe. He tugged at his collar and pulled it, stretching it, but still felt like it was choking him. He felt like someone stood on his chest, legs too heavy to move.

Roger took a chance and called Mark. He wanted to know if he should go to the hospital, if there was something really wrong with him, something he should worry about. Was this a heart attack? How were you supposed to know what a heart attack felt like before ever having one?

To his surprise, the doctor answered the phone. "Tell me where you are," he said after Roger's frantic rambling. "What's around?"

Roger continued to talk about his symptoms, his fear of death.

"Roger, tell me about the room. What's in the room?"

"It's a laundry room. There's nothing, just the washer and dryer and the soap machine," Roger forced out between struggling breaths.

"Put coins in the dryer, start it up. Trust me. Do it."

"What? Why? What are you saying?"

"Start the drier, Roger."

Roger fumbled in his pocket for quarters, then struggled to get them into the machine without dropping them. Without oxygen, his arms were going numb. Once he got the machine started, he collapsed to the floor. He was so frightened. What was happening?

"Okay. I can hear the machine. Focus on the door of the dryer. You see it tumbling, spinning? Which way is it going?"

"Clockwise."

"Keep watching it, listening to it tumble. Count how many times it goes around. Do it out loud. Let me hear you."

Roger did as he was told and before long, he found air again. Strength returned to his limbs. The pressure on his chest relented. "Am I okay? How did that work?"

He could almost see Mark's patented smile through the phone when the man gave a quiet chuckle. "You're okay. I have an opening at two o'clock. Come see me, and I'll explain it all to you. I'm glad you're feeling better."

"Alright. I'll see you at two." When Roger hung up, he continued to watch the tumbling drier until the time ran out and it stopped. Only then did he leave the laundry room and head back home.

15

JOINING THE CROWD, Roger moved with the flow of people through the doors of an open car nearby. Looking around, he found there to be no empty seats. It didn't take long. It never did. The subway was first come first served. As it so often was, the train car was overly packed with people. Anytime Roger rode the subway, he always wondered about the maximum occupancy. It seemed like a hazard the fire marshal would blow a gasket over if he were to see it and yet, it was commonplace for these city goers to be packed tightly into a tin can like so many sardines. Maybe there was someone running this city that was a sadist and secretly wanted them all to burn. The atmosphere brought back the anxiety he had just gotten rid of. It always did, but at least he knew it was temporary. He could focus on the stops. He would be off the train soon enough.

Roger grabbed onto a steel pole in the car's center to steady himself once the vehicle began its motion. It wasn't a smooth ride. It never was. The car rocked and rumbled, shaking and vibrating and tossing side to side. If you tried to just stand there without anything to hold onto, you would lose your footing. In a car so tightly packed with people, you were bound to anger whoever you landed on, never mind who you knocked them into. It would likely be a chain reaction of disaster that ended in blood shed.

Across and around him, many others found themselves in the

same position. Some just braced their palms on the ceiling to try to hold themselves in place, their faces displaying their obvious discomfort and dread, while others held onto chairbacks or other people who they hopefully came with and weren't violating but there was no way to tell with the subway crowd.

The doors slid closed, and the conductor listed the first stop over the intercom. Despite the volume of what seemed to be 10,000 decibels, the voice booming through the speakers still managed to be muffled and hardly audible as it crackled pertinent information.

Roger tried to think about what it was going to be like for him when he got back to his apartment. Would this be the last time? He didn't judge himself to be a very good person anymore anyway. The city did that to him. That building, Sunnycrest, did it to him. There was no coming back from what he'd done to the family across the hall. You couldn't just destroy a family and steal the life of an innocent child and carry on a righteous man.

The hell with it. The hell with it all. Part of him didn't care what was to happen and part of him was the same frightened child that ran from his father. Kara couldn't protect him from Alice like she had from their father. This was Roger's doing and only he could end it one way or another. As he rode the jostling subway train, he prayed for her forgiveness, but he didn't have faith in it.

Roger closed his eyes and shook his head at the thought. When he reopened them, he noticed her.

Alice.

She stood with the crowd at the far end of the car, watching him. She was only tall enough to reach most people's waists, and somehow, she didn't seem affected by the jerking sway of the rumbling train car. The ghost child did not bother with the balancing assistance of the thick pole at the center of the area she stood in. She held onto nothing but the filthy naked doll that always dangled from her hand, threads popping and arm threatening to come loose. As could be expected, Alice seemed way too preoccupied with Roger to be worried about losing her foot-ing. She was already dead. She could probably do whatever she wanted.

Roger's hands started to sweat upon the sight of her. He slid them up to a higher place on the pole. The metal was cold and dry and would keep him from slipping, at least for the time being. He just hoped he didn't need to move them again as so many other hands were wrapped around the pole as well. He didn't think the people around him would take kindly to him putting his hand on theirs. They would surely take that the entirely wrong way. Then he would have more than the ghost to contend with and his father was proof he was no more coura-geous with the living than he was the dead.

Gripping the pole much tighter than he needed to, Roger watched the little girl, vengeance swelling in the dark pits of her eyes as she stood firm, not swayed by the rocking motion of the car. The black veins moved across her face, changing shape as if they were snakes that lived beneath her pale, icy flesh, stretching and retracting.

Roger swallowed hard and raised his gaze from her to those who unknowingly accompanied her, as blindly unaware of her presence as the taxi driver had been.

If only they knew, he thought. He wished he could somehow join them in their blissful ignorance. Roger would have given anything at that moment to be so blindly unaware of the ghost in the car, but she wasn't there for any of them. She was there for *him*.

Roger didn't just see the girl in the car with him. He could feel her presence within him. The two of them were connected.

Just let me get home, he thought. *We'll finish then, however you wish. Just let me get home.*

He wished he could tell himself she was the boogeyman, a nightmarish child's fantasy that wasn't real. But he couldn't, not after today. Not after everything.

Alice was real.

She was real, and she was there inside the train car with him. The train was moving, sealed doors on every side. He felt like an animal caged with its natural predator.

Roger's eyes moved back to Alice as she slowly raised her left arm. It moved stiffly, almost mechanically, like the limited motion of a lifeless department store mannequin. The right arm remained at her side, still holding that damned doll, its own arm tearing enough to show the stuffing within. Her movement was stiff and rigid, like she was an opposable action figure being positioned accordingly. Once her arm was fully extended in his direction, her index finger flipped outward, like it was spring activated, jutting from her small hand accusingly. She stood that way, the train rocking around her unperturbed form, pointing at him accusingly.

Roger gasped and forced himself to look away from her, but he talked to her silently within his mind. *Yes. I'm guilty. It's all my fault. I get it. Just let me get home. Please. Just wait and do this at Sunnycrest. I know you hate me. You have every right to hate me. Just... wait.*

Pinning his eyes on the doors of the train, he watched the dull scenery pass by through the portal-like windows. Out of the corner of his eye, he could still see her—or at least the shape of her small form—pointing in his direction. He could feel her stare crawling over him like the worms that poured from her mouth, slipping along his flesh, and giving him goosebumps.

Roger swallowed a lump in his throat. *Just let me make it home.*

He tapped his foot nervously, a habit he'd had since he was a small child. He waited for the train to come to a stop so he could run. He was silently begging the brakes to work their magic, praying for the doors to open. He no longer cared about the other people on the train. He was prepared to shove them all out of his way or climb over their backs if he had to. Screw them.

Roger knew it was foolish and Alice wasn't his father. She wasn't something he could run away from, but he was overtaken by fear and his old instincts kicked in. It was human instinct:

fight or flight mode. His gut screamed at him to run, to flee. The next stop was not his stop, but he was ready to run now, to hit the streets above like he had just stolen a purse. Roger shivered despite the hot, stuffy, over-packed car. Peripheral vision let him watch as Alice's arm stiffly lowered back to her side. He almost sighed with relief.

"Come on. Come on," he said quietly, mumbling under his breath, as he forced his eyes not to look away from the car doors. "Open. Open. Open."

The compulsion to look her direction grew more intense as he spied her taking a step forward. Roger's leg tapping became more rapid, almost furious, as his nerves accelerated, which earned him dirty looks from the people surrounding him as they were forced to share the pole with his trembling form.

"Can you stop?" one person asked him.

Roger ignored the complaint. Alice took another step toward him, and he felt like he was going to completely lose it. "Don't look. Don't look," he told himself. He repeated it like a mantra.

The other passengers stared daggers at him. People left the pole he clutched to move elsewhere despite the lack of room, stumbling and falling into others while issuing apologies. They would rather take their chances falling on or annoying their fellow passengers than stay by the crazy man who was shaking, tapping, and mumbling to himself.

Screw it. Go.

Roger fought against turning his head as she took another step in his direction. His heart pounded, slamming against the walls of his chest as if it were wrongly imprisoned. It felt almost like there was some form of magnetic pull drawing him to look at her. It was like it had been out on the street, like some force or invisible hand tried to force him to do its bidding, pushing his head, twisting his neck, but he fought against it. He had to remain in control. He thought about the strong people he knew, people like Kara and Mark.

"Don't look. Don't look," Roger continued to repeat, in what he was well aware to be a futile effort. His attempt at gaining control of the situation was silly and pointless, yet he still felt compelled to try. It was some kind of internal survival instinct sewn into his consciousness. It was primal. His nature as a human was to fight back, regardless of the odds.

He didn't know what Alice's true intention was, but it felt like life or death to him. For all he knew, maybe it was. He hadn't been caught yet to find out what would happen if he was. He didn't plan on finding out anytime soon either, at least not before he made it back to Sunnycrest. If she wanted to have a final showdown within the walls of that terrible place, then she was welcome to bring it, but he wasn't going to stand by and let it happen here on her terms.

"Seriously. Do you mind?" another passenger, standing next to him in the cramped car asked, their voice flooded with irritation. They punctuated the statement by moving their eyes down to his rapidly tapping foot and shaking leg.

"Right. Sorry," Roger said with a forced half smile, his brow beaded with sweat. "I don't know why I do that. Nervous habit." His façade of calmness was easily seen through. His words stumbled out of his mouth drunkenly, and his voice was unsteady. It was impossible for him to portray any level of sincerity at this point. The other man groaned and rolled his eyes, but he didn't move away like so many others had.

Roger's nerves may have the best of him, but he tried his damnedest to keep his leg under control. He didn't want to make more of a scene than he already had, at least not before those doors opened. On the other hand, maybe it was good if he got the other passengers to avoid him, as it would clear his path to freedom. Salvation laid in the open air beyond those doors. At least for the moment.

Alice stepped forward again with her left foot. Then slowly, like dragging a ball and chain behind her, she slid right up alongside it. Roger could hear it drag, a sound like sandpaper scraped against itself.

Roger couldn't stand it anymore. This was another game, and he was bound to lose as he lost them all, so he just threw in the towel to forfeit. He turned to face the dead child as she repeated the process.

Left foot stomp.

Right foot drag.

The sound of the dragging limb was like fingernails on a chalkboard to him. It made his skin crawl. He remembered how her leg broke.

Roger had the dead girl in his arms, her own arm hanging limply over his. This was the worst moment of his life. It was an accident, a horrible accident but would anyone believe that? He wasn't the monster. Brian was the monster. He was just like Roger's dad, worse maybe. Roger tried to save the girl, to do what no one did for him, to help her get away. It just went so horribly wrong.

He had listened to the yelling, the way Alice screamed back at her father the same way Kara had when they were children. He knew what happened to Kara after those moments, even if he was long gone when it happened. He would see the bruises when she found him cowering in the woods. Now Alice had paid the final price and it was at Roger's hands, but at least she wasn't broken. She was peaceful. She looked like she was sleeping.

Unfortunately, the beast was still lurking about, stomping and shouting, frantically searching for her. Roger had to get her out of the building in a hurry. He planned to take the back stairs, to avoid as many eyes as possible. The truth was, he wanted to avoid Brian most of all. He imagined his father running through those halls, screaming his name instead of Alice's. He knew it wasn't real, but he couldn't shake it.

He ran with the child in his arms, racing for the stairwell. He heard the ding of the elevator behind him and panicked. He dove forward, slipping through the stairwell door as it slammed shut, but he'd misjudged. Alice's leg hit the wall and bent awkwardly. Then the door slammed shut on it. The small bones crunched, and Roger grit his teeth to keep from crying out. Tears immediately formed in his wide eyes. He pried the heavy door open to free her and stared at the misshapen form of her small leg as it slammed shut without obstruction. He jumped at the *bang!*

"I'm so sorry," he whispered as he made his way down toward the waiting car. "I'm so sorry for everything."

16

AT THE HOSPITAL, they believed the broken leg was proof of her father's abuse. But Alice knew the truth, and it seemed Roger was done getting away with it. It was another accidental crime he committed against her; another part of his giant lies.

Alice was only a few feet away now. Roger hadn't realized how close she had gotten while he was lost in the memories of his own guilt. He was sweating profusely now, to the point where it was difficult to hold onto the pole any longer. He wanted to scream, to demand she leave at once despite the fact he knew she wouldn't listen. He had no leverage, nothing to threaten her with. The power was all hers, and she knew it. They both knew it.

Roger wanted to back up, but the train car was full and there was simply nowhere to back up to. Tears welled in his eyes. He didn't even realize when he stopped breathing all together. The unbreakable magnetism glued his eyes to the quickly rotting corpse of the still moving, dead child as she shifted her left foot forward again, dropping it in place hard like a lead weight. Roger could hear the resonating bang of its collision with the metal floor of the car.

Alice's right foot dragged itself forward again and seemed to have resistance she had to force the leg against, like she was fighting against gravity. The foot came with a loud scraping noise that reminded Roger of the squealing brakes of the train.

The lights in the car started to flicker on and off. No one else seemed to hear the squeal of her dragging her dead limb, but they did all look around as the lights took on a mind of their own. It was proof enough for him that Alice was real, and the haunting wasn't just in his mind. He wasn't telekinetic. He couldn't flicker the lights with his guilt and shame.

If this train didn't stop soon, she was going to get him, and there would be nothing he could do about it. Roger had no way to know what that would entail, but he knew enough to be frightened. The terror ran deep enough he swore he could feel it in his bones, like fingernails scraping down to his marrow.

If she did get him, then surely everyone would see and hear something, he thought. If they could see the lights flashing on and off, they couldn't ignore if he was gutted alive by an invisible force before their eyes in a train car they couldn't escape from.

The left foot again.

Thump.

The right.

The lights continued, faster now. On. Off. On. Off.

The speed of the flickering quickened, matching his anxiety-ridden heartbeat as he faced the dread, the inevitability, of his demise. Alice was almost upon him. It would be over soon. Roger knew in his heart he deserved it, but he still didn't want it. He couldn't handle knowing it was going to happen, anticipating it. He wanted to scream, to cry, to beg for her mercy. Would he once she reached him? He didn't know the answer and he didn't want to find out.

The brakes of the train squealed then, like the screams of the dying. Roger's eyes darted from the dead girl back to the doors of the train car. Maybe he could still make it out alive. *Open. Open. Open. Goddammit. Open!*

The left foot.

Thump.

The right.

Screeeeeeeeeee!

The train car jerked to a sudden stop, almost knocking unprepared people over in the commotion of the flickering overhead lights. Roger's leg started going again, and he made no attempt to stop it this time. He couldn't possibly have cared less whether or not he was inconveniencing the man next to him or any of the others for that matter. To hell with common courtesy. This was a matter of life and death, and both fates were a moment away. It was a matter of which came first. *Come on. Come on. Come on.*

The left foot.

Thump!

The right foot.

Screeeeeeeeeee!

Alice was in front of him, cavernous eye sockets staring forward, pinning themselves to him, maggots crawling lazily over the edges to fall onto her black dress and shoes.

He gripped the big, steel pole like he was the dead one and rigor mortis had set in. It was the only thing between them, and it didn't ease his mind in the slightest. Roger didn't have much faith in the guardianship of the metal cylinder. Alice was dead. What was a pole going to do to stop her? She had already proved she could be anywhere she wanted to be, that she could disappear and reappear and slow time at her will. The pole offered him no safety. If she wanted him, she would have him. His speeding heart suddenly seized like it had stopped its beating all together. His breath ceased as well. He was just waiting for her to do whatever it was she was going to do. He was powerless to do anything but wait.

Go on. Do it.

Roger watched as her arm rose again. It moved slower than humanly possible, but time seemed to wait for it, like the arm was in control, not the universe.

Finally, it came to a stop outright, fist extended toward his face. His jaw clenched as he stared down at the undead girl's small white hand, covered in the bruises of broken blood vessels and clotted blood beneath her thin skin.

Then the lights went out completely.

Darkness fell over the train car.

People murmured in the pitch black, starting to feel their own level of anxiety or at least annoyance.

Roger didn't move. He didn't breathe. He just waited.

The lights came back on and Alice's spring-loaded index finger popped out again, pointed right at his face, in tandem with the opening doors of the train car, the sound of the sliding doors fitting perfectly as if they were the sound effect of her moving finger.

Roger screamed. He couldn't keep it in any longer. It broke away from him like a caged animal desperate for freedom tearing through a rusted gate.

Alice didn't move. She didn't even twitch. She just stood there like the mere statue of a child, pointing at him accusingly. Her finger poised with judgment at his face. Somehow, he could feel it, the presence of it, despite the fact she was too small in stature for that finger to actually reach him.

Passengers started to exit the train. None of them seemed in much of a hurry. They grumbled under their breaths about the lights and the crazy guy. Roger watched them move by him, so relaxed and effortless, and he felt ready to explode. His whole body shook with the tremors of impending madness.

Roger's eyes moved back to the statue-like little girl he once held in his arms. He saw her then as the girl he had killed, the girl he had murdered. He saw her behind his eyes as he carried her body down those stairs toward his car, apologizing to her motionless form as he went.

Her eyes returned then, filling the empty sockets with emerald green irises that wavered so terribly sad. Her gaze alone was pleading with him for her life back, and at once, the guilt rose up in him like vomit in his throat. It was overwhelming and boiled over the brim of his pot of sanity. Tears burst from his eyes in rushing tides, and he screamed, "Move!"

Then he was in motion, pushing, shoving, knocking everyone out of his path. They screamed and cursed at him, threatening him with bodily harm and lawsuits in equal measure, but he paid them no attention. When his feet touched down on the platform, he paid one last glance toward the inside of the train. The dead girl didn't change position or even move her feet. She just rotated like she was a music box ballerina, until her pointing finger faced him again. Her green eyes fell away, popping free from her rotting skull to leave behind the empty accusatory sockets as the eyeballs rolled across the floor of the train car to the open doors and disappeared into the gap.

Roger stumbled backward, tripped over someone's luggage, and tumbled painfully to the ground. He cried out. Roger grew suddenly wild, the cocktail of fear and guilt proving beyond his tolerance. He hurled the suitcase away with a growl, in a hurry to get back to his feet. The owner of the luggage's complaints went unheard, at least by him.

If they tried to stop him, he probably would have thrown them just the same. They were far less threatening than what was behind him and what was inside him. He knew the truth. He was running from what he had done, running from himself, from the ramifications of his trauma. It changed nothing. The knowledge of this truth didn't still his legs.

Roger ran. He ran for the steps, then up to the street and this time he didn't look back at all. He didn't even stop when he broke free of the subway into the more natural gloom of the coming night. He hit the pavement and kept right on going. There was no stopping now, no slowing, no tricks to help him with the maddening anxiety that had now taken the wheel. He didn't let his anxiety fill his mind with thoughts of the past. He didn't think at all. He just ran. Roger ran, and he kept on running, and he didn't stop until he had made it all the way home, all the way to the Sunnycrest Apartments, to the place where this all began.

17

"THIS IS IT," Roger thought, looking up at the massive stone creation. "This is home."

He never thought much about it when he first moved there. He paid it no mind really. It was old, worn, and more than a little creepy, but it was also cheap, convenient, and perfect, according to Kara.

Roger saw it so differently now after a day of facing his demons, running from Alice, and running from himself. He could never rush inside without a care like he used to when Alice was alive, when she was just a reflection of his own childhood. Every time he faced the outside of the building now, he felt strangely compelled to stand there, look at it, take it in, bask in its power, and see it clearly.

Sunnycrest was huge and intimidating, foreboding, and menacing. It was alive. There was an electric current that radiated from the old stones that compiled it. He couldn't explain it, but he could feel it, a tingling sensation under his skin. If it was possible for a man-made structure to have an aura, then this one surely did, and Roger had a feeling it wasn't good. The building wasn't a victim, a house infiltrated by spirits, taken over and overthrown. Sunnycrest was more like their master, a demon built of stone, calling them forth from wherever they came. *Come to me*.

The bizarre energy that emanated from the building itself,

from the stone to the foundation had always been there. Roger had just been too pre-occupied to notice it before, but it was always there, touching him like the fingers of a ghostly hand.

Roger had always seen the recognition of it on the faces of visitors, people that didn't live within the walls and weren't cogs in the supernatural machine. People looked disturbed, frightened, even ashamed, as if they had been molested somehow, violated by the presence of the building, but they never spoke of it. It was painted on their faces like a macabre mask, or choreographed in the abused way they carried themselves, victims as they were. They would arrive happy and leave looking different, broken.

Roger had been watching out the window, waiting with childlike anticipation for the delivery of a package. It wasn't coming from the postman. He had already come and gone. He bit his lip and drummed his fingers on the windowsill.

His mother had found his old sketchbook from high school, his yearbook, and some other things that were all tied to memories. She had put them in a box and shipped them over to him. He had forgotten all about how much he used to love to draw. He had wanted to be a comic book artist at one point. If he had known then that he would end up a half-assed salesman with an associate degree, he may have actually pursued it.

His eyes lit up like a child's on Christmas morning when he saw the big delivery truck pull to a stop out front. He smiled gleefully and clapped his hands. He ran for the door. Delivery guys tended to leave packages by the mailboxes downstairs rather then bring them up to the appropriate floor. He didn't think anyone would steal his old sketchbook, but he still wanted to get down there right away.

Roger hurried to the elevator, tugging his phone from his pocket, and calling Kara as he did. He got into the elevator and hit the button for the lobby as he told Kara what his mother had found. "She said there's more. I can only imagine. You should come by after work and check it out."

"That definitely sounds like fun, Rodge. I'll bring popcorn."

Roger laughed and moved before the doors were even fully open, rushing out onto the first floor. He saw his package and wanted to thank the person who left it.

"I'll see you then!" he said before returning his phone to his pocket. His eyes moved toward the front door, and he saw the man in his delivery uniform heading toward it. Roger called to him and raised an arm, waving his thanks.

The man turned back, but he wasn't looking at Roger. He was staring toward a closed door, one of the first-floor apartments. Roger was confused by the man's odd behavior. He scooped up his package and headed toward the man who dropped it off, the man who still seemed to not even notice him.

"Hey, you okay?" Roger called as he approached. "Thanks for the delivery. I've been waiting for it. I really appreciate it."

The man slowly turned as if he recognized Roger's presence for the first time. His eyes looked distant, hollow, and full of grief and fear. His mouth quivered like he wanted to speak but couldn't find the words.

Roger gave a nervous chuckle. "Hey, you okay, man? You look like you saw a ghost or something."

The man just blinked. A single tear rolled from his left eye. Then he turned on his heel and left the building. Roger watched him head down the walkway toward his truck. The man never looked back. It was the strangest thing.

Roger shook his head and took his package back upstairs to open it.

18

ROGER DIDN'T REALIZE THEN that the only tenants he had ever seen leave the building in the time he had been there, really leave—leave and never come back to it—had not left of their own free will. They were either committed, imprisoned, or dead. It made him almost as afraid to move out of Sunnycrest as he was to stay there with Alice. He thought about it as he stood by that beautiful big tree and stared at the front of the building.

"Couldn't it just be that people don't leave because they're happy?"

Roger turned around and saw Ben, the gay man from floor five who worked as a drag queen at a late-night diner downtown. The man smiled and waved at him.

Roger gave him a confused look. "Excuse me? How did you know what I was thinking?"

Ben laughed. "How do you not know the difference between thinking and talking, honey? Thinking is supposed to happen *inside* your head. Anyway, I'm just saying, people are reluctant to leave a good thing, you know? Not everything needs to be something ominous."

Roger watched the laughing man head past him to the front door.

"Am I holding this for you?" Ben asked, looking back.

Roger shook his head. "No. That's fine. Thank you. I'm gonna hang here for a moment."

"Suit yourself. But I think you're hanging with the wrong crowd. What is she, seven? It's a little weird man."

Ben went inside and let the door fall shut behind him. The door was heavy and closed hard like an exclamation point to his alarming statement.

Roger's mouth fell open, but Ben was no longer there. He looked around for the child Ben had seen him with. For once, he was the one who didn't see her. Why did she show sometimes and not others? Why did her face change? Her hair and clothes? Was it intentional? It was an everchanging game, and Alice was the only one who knew the rules.

He turned in a circle, his eyes combing the front yard and coming back to the big tree. He thought back to Alice being happy again. Is that how Ben saw her just now? It had to be right? He would have had more of a reaction if he had seen her the way Roger had on the train. Roger took a deep breath and looked back at the tall building looming before him.

Roger thought about what Ben had said. Not about Alice. The other thing. If the building was evil, people would talk about it, wouldn't they? No one had warned him when he moved in. No one had come screaming from another apartment and begged him to save himself and told him to run away and not sign the lease. Surely they would have if the place was evil, right? At least one of them? Maybe they were all happy, content with the low rent and good location. Maybe. But even if that was true, Roger couldn't join them in their contentment. Maybe there were two sides to the building, and he was unlucky enough to see the dark side.

"When I get upstairs, we gotta talk," he said, hoping Alice could hear him. He didn't expect a response, so he wasn't bothered when he didn't get one. He just nodded, his eyes returning to the bricks that housed the ghosts. He thought to when he had tried to do his part and warn Sarah, the girl moving into the vacancy on floor two.

Roger heard Alice. She was giggling and talking to that damned doll of hers. He heard her little feet pouncing around his living room, but he saw nothing. He told himself she was harmless, but he was starting to feel differently. It felt like he had a stalker, someone who was always around, following him, watching him, and fully intent on making him crazy.

Through his window, he saw the building manager walking up with a young Asian girl. He hadn't seen the girl before and felt suddenly nervous, afraid for her. Was she coming to live here? He shook his head. He couldn't let the innocent young lady move into this building of torment.

Roger pulled himself from the window and crossed to his front door. When he opened it, something fell and crashed behind him. He cringed but didn't turn to look. It was just more evidence that something was wrong with this place, that the dead didn't leave.

He hurried to the elevator and frantically pushed the down button.

An old woman standing beside him with curls of blue hair said with a smile, "Are you sure it's not just your ghost? Maybe it's you that's haunted, not the building."

"What?" Roger said, turning to face her. He gasped when he found himself alone in the hallway. The doors opened and he hurried into the elevator. *Come on. Come on.* His eyes watched the numbers, waiting nervously to reach the lobby.

When the doors came open, he rushed out into the new hall. The building manager, Gary, who ran things for his mother Agatha, was talking to the girl Roger had seen from his window.

"Now there's two laundry rooms," Gary told the girl. "One on this floor, and one on floor seven. Odd I know, but you're free to use whichever you want."

"This building is haunted," Roger said, hurrying over. "You shouldn't sign the lease. It's not safe."

The young woman's eyes grew large. "What? Who are you?"

Gary glared at Roger and steered the woman toward the first-floor laundry room and away from Roger. "I'm sorry, Sarah," he said. "That man lives on floor seven and he doesn't come down much anymore. You won't see him unless you need to buy business supplies. He works sales for Grander Milton and Co."

Roger stood outside the laundry room and listened as Sarah responded, "I'm just a student so I won't need business supplies for a few years. If that guy is on floor seven, I think I'll stick to this laundry room."

Roger took a deep breath and walked with a slouch back to the elevator. He went up to his place where he waited for the knock on the door he knew was coming. He answered with a frown when it came.

"I'm sorry," Roger said.

"Me too," Gary answered. "If you try to scare off other tenants, I'm going to have to ask you to leave, Roger."

Roger nodded his understanding. "It won't happen again."

"I hope not, and I hope you made enough commission to actually pay your rent this month...in full."

"I'm trying," Roger said.

"We all are," Gary told him before walking off down the hall.

"We all are," Alice's voice said mockingly from nowhere.

Roger simply sighed.

19

ROGER WISHED HE COULD MOVE. He had been looking. Kara was helping him too, cutting ads out and keeping an eye open for signs, but most places in the city were well above his price range. The moment he could figure out how to resolve things with Alice, he wanted to have somewhere to go. That was his goal, to make amends then leave her haunting the halls of Sunnycrest for the people like Sarah who didn't heed his warning, and to move on and start fresh somewhere else, preferably out of the city altogether.

So far, his plan wasn't going well. If he didn't get his sales up, he wasn't sure he was even going to have a job. It was hard to think or plan anything when Alice wouldn't stop harassing him. That's why he needed to end this, to face her and end this one way or another, which started with actually entering this building.

Roger surveyed the massive structure before him. He looked it over, analyzing it, maybe because he was stalling or maybe just out of fearful respect. He knew he should be running inside, charging up to his apartment and confronting Alice, but he couldn't; not yet.

Roger couldn't cross the threshold until he had traced the cracks of the walls, the words scrawled in graffiti, the chips in the bricks, the bloodstains of those the building had already fed upon. The stains had faded over time and become one with the wall now, some of them age old, but if you really looked, you could still see them. This was the evidence of the building's power, proof that it consumes you, quite literally. The blood and marrow of the past residents were the mortar between the bricks that strengthened the walls.

Roger acknowledged the kudzu that had grown into the wall, attaching Sunnycrest to the eaerth. He felt as much as saw the shadows of the residents at the windows looking out at him with silent affirmation. All the letters remained in the welcome sign , but the lights were failing, and they blinked on and off like some form of Morse code, the word Sunnycrest flashing ominously. The grounds around the building were well taken care of, but the groundskeeper was consistently planting new flowers as they didn't seem able to survive for some reason. Roger thought that Sunnycrest stole all life, not just human life. It was probably irrational but it was the reason he didn't get a pet despite how badly he needed company and comfort.

The groundskeeper, a man named Willie, seemed to know the truth of the building. He kept to himself and didn't speak much, but he always stopped working to look at the people that lived there like he was grieving for them, as if he saw their terrible future and the end that fate had in store for them. Roger tried to start a conversation with the man shortly after he moved to Sunnycrest.

Willie was a short man, built stocky like a boxer. He maintained a tan all year round. No matter how often the plants died, he never gave up. Willie was always out there working tirelessly. Roger had a lot of respect for the man, and he wanted to know more about him. Besides, Mark had been telling him that he needed to talk to people, to try to make connections. He jokingly called it homework so who better to start with than the man who worked on his home.

"Hi there. Roger. Apartment 34."

Willie stared at him with big, sympathetic eyes, then carried on planting a new set of flowers in the garden out front. Roger waited and shuffled his feet, but no further response came. When Roger finally shrugged and walked away, the groundskeeper spoke from behind him.

He said, "I learned when I first started working here to never talk to dead people."

Roger raised a lone eyebrow and looked back at him quizzically. "Well, I assure you, sir, that I am very much alive."

"Only on the outside," Willie said back. "Not a whole lotta difference between you and them."

"Them?"

Apparently, the conversation was over as Willie's focus was back on his gardening.

With a sigh, Roger entered the building.

20

ROGER HAD TAKEN old Willie for a madman that day and made a mental note not to talk to him anymore, which he stuck to, but now, after all he'd been through with Alice, he thought back on that conversation and realized old Willie had known exactly what was happening at Sunnycrest. Roger had been the fool.

The limbs of the big tree at the right front side of the building, where Roger had sat watching Alice that day, shaded the entrance. The front of the tree had a heart with the letters RJ and KT carved into it. Sometimes when he was bored, Roger would sit around and try to imagine the story behind that, because he knew there had to be one, a childhood love, two dreamers believing they would be together forever. Maybe they were. And maybe they were ghosts walking the halls of Sunnycrest hand in hand. Before he approached the front door, Roger traced his fingers over the crude carving.

"Are you still here?" he wondered. "Are you still alive?"

Then he shook it off. Roger looked at the front door, as if it were beckoning him, wondering what was taking him so long. The wind made the old door sway back and forth. Every fourth swing, it would loudly bang into the wall. It did this all the time, yet it still made him jump and shiver. Swallowing hard, Roger started down the stone walkway toward the creaking, swinging door. His guard was up as if the door were a strange dog that may attack him as he passed by. Roger's paranoia was getting the best of him. This had gone beyond anxiety now.

"This is what you're doing to me," he said to Alice, though he still failed to see her. "You're making me crazy."

A child's laughter sounded behind him. Roger felt someone standing next to him. He looked to his left and found the old lady he had seen by the elevator the day he tried to warn Sarah.

"It's not really fair to blame the child," she said. "You were always a little crazy."

Roger closed his eyes and counted to ten. When he opened them, the lady was gone. He took a deep breath and nodded to himself.

Licking his dry lips, he said out loud, "Let's get this over with."

Then he didn't wait any longer. There would be no drifting into memories, no anxious questioning, no more stalling. Roger grabbed the heavy door before it could bang open again and made his way into the building.

21

THE BURGUNDY CARPET that led the way into the Sunnycrest Apartments stretched through the entire first floor hall all the way to the back door. It was the tongue to the mouth of madness and Roger walked right in. He was thankful there weren't teeth to go with it.

The walls creaked on their own, and the dimming lights swung like lame limbs from the ceiling, creaking as they moved. "Welcome home," it seemed to say in its own twisted way.

The building didn't need words to speak to its inhabitants. It groaned, clicked, and buzzed its greetings and farewells. Roger heard a squeak nearby and looked over to see a small field mouse eyeing him from within one of the built-in heating vents. As soon as he acknowledged the small creature, he heard the giant furnace kick on and a blast of heat cooked the rodent before it could flee. The smell was awful and molested his sinuses.

A thin, Hispanic man exited Apartment 5 when it happened. He looked at Roger and frowned. "It's sad how the building does things like that, just to be cruel." Then he turned toward the wall as if he were talking to the building itself. "You cooked that critter while we were watching, just to display your power. We all already know. It's unnecessary and just plain mean."

Roger listened to the man chastise the building for bad behavior, and it sent a chill scurrying over him like the ghost of the mouse that had just died. Roger paled at the thought. In this building, that might have been exactly what it was.

With a deep breath, Roger headed over toward the waiting elevator. About halfway there, he heard something crunch under his foot and stopped in his tracks, closing his eyes and sighing. When he reopened them, he saw a pink plastic asthma inhaler laying broken at his feet.

Roger's heart jumped and his hands trembled. He told himself it was a coincidence; anyone in the building could be asthmatic. It didn't have to belong to Alice, but somehow, he knew that it did.

He looked at the man who had disciplined the building a moment ago. "Mr. Martinez, did you see anyone drop an inhaler over here by the elevator?"

The thin man looked his way as he used his key to lock his door. "I just came out myself, but if I had to guess, I'd say it was that little girl that's always following you around this place. Wasn't she asthmatic?" He patted Roger on the arm as he walked by and made his way out the front door.

"I'm sorry. I didn't see it," Roger said to Alice. "You don't need it anymore, do you? I hope you don't. That seems unfair. You should be able to not worry about stuff like that anymore, I think." Either way, he had broken the inhaler, and he owed her an apology for that. "Still, sorry I broke it. I'm sorry I'm still finding ways to accidentally harm you."

Sighing then, Roger stepped over the broken plastic pieces and crossed the last few feet to the elevator. He reached out with a shaking hand and clicked the faded *up* button. Then he waited, growing more anxious by the second. He felt vulnerable out there in the open hall, like he was going to be cooked like the mouse.

Roger could hear labored breathing as he waited for the elevator to arrive. It seemed to come from every direction. Was it his fault for stepping on the inhaler? Was it Alice letting him know how he was still making her suffer, killing her all over again? Maybe it was the building itself, toying with him. Sunnycrest was the only real witness to what had happened with Alice in the laundry room that day. The building saw everything. It knew his guilt. It knew Alice was still hanging around as well. Maybe it had invited her; let her in somehow.

It's just a building, Roger. A building. That's all. Nothing else. You're the one that's haunted.

The elevator stopped with a ding. Roger watched intensely as the old doors shook and rattled, writhing in seeming agony as they struggled to slide open and provide him with access. One day this elevator was going to swallow someone and collapse into the bowels of this beast. He just hoped he was not the one inside at the time.

Stepping inside the elevator, Roger pressed the seven button and stepped away from the rickety doors as they proceeded to go through their painful movement again, screaming in agony as they did. The steel box lurched hard before it started its ascent. Roger grimaced as an overwhelming nervousness hit him. He was not sure if it was fear of what awaited him on the seventh floor or if it was the fear of not making it there and succumbing to a worse fate while trapped in this death box. He found himself shaking and sweating with nervous tension once again. This was becoming the story of his life. He was barely functioning as a human being anymore.

Staring up at the slowly rising numbers, he thought taking the stairs would have been faster. Faster wasn't the issue though. In the elevator, nothing could sneak up behind him. It was lit well, as the lights were one of the only things about the elevator that worked properly, unlike the stairwell which basically had no working lights at all, and what lights it did have were as dim as humanly possible. Then there was the bitter truth that Roger didn't want to climb all the way up to the seventh floor. Stress had a way of physically exhausting him. His body ached and his muscles felt weary.

As he looked up, waiting to see the number three light up

ever so dimly, he felt something tug at his pant leg. Without looking, he slid his hand down his leg to feel at the spot. Nothing was there, but as soon as he moved his hand away, he could feel the tugging resume. He shivered.

This time, Roger looked, but he still found nothing. His eyes just saw his pant leg, though the fabric did look ruffled as if it had been grabbed by a small hand. Roger was alone in the world's slowest moving elevator as far as he could tell, but he knew better. Why was she showing herself to other people but not to him now?

With a deep breath, he looked up in time to finally see the three light up in full. He exhaled and waited impatiently for the four as the tugging at his leg resumed once again. He brushed at his leg with growing frustration, but the tugging continued.

Lowering his eyes ever so slightly, Roger looked into the warped reflection of himself in the rusty steel doors ahead. There was the vague blurry image of a small girl standing next to him. He watched with horror as she tugged at his pants leg with her pale hand. The image was skewed and made him feel like he was looking into a fun house mirror, depicting him and Alice standing together like a father and daughter, waiting for their floor together.

Trying not to move, he turned his head ever so slightly and rolled his eyes to view the steel wall to his left where the girl was standing in the doors' reflection. The walls were not as rusted as the doors and the image of Alice standing at his side was much clearer and easier to view. She was looking up at him, her face stern and hateful, as she tugged hard at his leg.

Even if this had been the average elevator, moving at the usual pace, it wouldn't have been moving fast enough for him now that he was aware of his current company. Roger was on his way up to talk to Alice, but he still didn't want to be closed in this tiny box with her. He found it suddenly difficult to breathe. He wanted to have space to run, to hide, if it didn't go well, to get away if need be.

"I'm sorry," he said without looking down at where he knew she was standing.

Alice didn't respond. She just continued on as she was, small hand fiercely gripping the leg of his pants. Why was she doing this to him? Hadn't she seen him suffering all this time? Didn't she know how tormented he had been ever since that day, how broken he was inside because of what had happened? Why couldn't she just forgive him? Even if she did, the truth was he would still never forgive himself. She had to know that. Didn't she know that?

"Don't you know that?" he said out loud.

Roger looked up to see the five was lit now. He frowned, wishing it had been the seven so he could get off this thing. His gaze moved down to the refection in the door, and he spied her, still standing there at his side. Alice's head turned slowly to face him as if she knew he were watching.

"I'm sorry," he said again, honestly. "You have no idea how sorry I am. I need you to believe that."

Alice's nose began to bleed then, black blood spilling over her pale face as she stared back at him with hard eyes, in the refection of the door. She yanked on his pants leg, pulling him off balance. Roger yelped. He didn't mean to. It was a knee jerk reaction. If she was trying to tell him something, he had no idea what it was. The image on the doors had become less visible. The metal of the doors had fogged up, as if someone had purposely breathed onto it. Roger turned his head to look at the wall. Alice was still beside him clutching at his pants. When he turned back, it looked to him as if someone had used their finger to write a message in the fog. Was it someone else or was Alice able to be in two places at once?

Across the elevator door, it said, "Not."

The elevator stopped with another fierce lurching movement. The tugging at his leg stopped in time with it. Roger took a deep breath as the doors rattled and whined in their attempt to open for him. Even though he had been in a hurry to arrive at this floor, he suddenly felt reluctant to step out of the metal box.

Roger rubbed his sweaty palms on his shirt as he watched the doors working their hardest to open for him. He imagined them a feeble old man that refused to give up his independence although he wasn't really capable of doing things anymore. The doors would have given him anxiety on a good day. Standing beside Alice, he felt ready to lose his mind.

When they finally succeeded in their geriatric mission and parted so he could make his way through, he saw Alice go running past him, bounding down the hallway, giggling and chasing her big rubber ball, doll in hand. She looked alive again, happy.

Roger's breath caught in his chest, and he stumbled backward into the elevator. Waiting, his heart pounding, he saw nothing else. His eyes ran back and forth across the hallway just as the child had. Hesitantly, he approached the open doors. Before moving through them, Roger poked his head out and looked around the corner. He didn't see her at the end of the hall even though he had just watched her run that way.

He knew she wasn't gone though. She was there. She was still with him. She was always with him, like Mr. Martinez had so kindly reminded him. He just couldn't see her. He could feel her though. He had that feeling of being watched, that feeling that he wasn't alone.

Where are you? Are you in the apartment waiting for me?

Just to be safe, Roger turned his head and looked the other direction. He didn't see her there either. The hallway was empty and quiet aside from the faint sound of rock music playing in someone's apartment at least three doors down. Feeling safe for the moment, he took another deep breath, then faced forward again. When he did, Alice stood directly in front of him staring at him with those pitch black, cavernous eyes, a stern look on her face. The emerald of her eyes was missing, her color and life gone, the rot returned.

Roger jumped, crying out in fear. He fell into the elevator, loudly crashing down on his backside. The rusty old box voiced its complaints by whining and swaying. In his mind, he pictured it coming loose and flying down to the bottom, unrestrained, to smash him to bits.

From his place on the ground, he looked up at Alice. A smile creased her blue-tinged lips and she reached into the elevator with a pale hand. He noticed the nail on the middle finger was missing. It was just raw flesh. Her smiled widened to show him her teeth. They were pearly white and in perfect contrast with the rest of her. Then she pushed the button for the lobby and backed out of the elevator.

"What are you doing?" he asked, but the doors didn't seem to have any trouble moving this time. They slammed shut in an instant, cutting off his view of the dead girl.

The jerking lurch of the steel box seemed almost violent now as if the building had gotten angry for some reason. The movement threw him into the left wall as he worked to get to his feet. Tears rose in his eyes. She was going to use the elevator to kill him after all. She was going to take his life in return for him taking hers. He owed her that. Roger wasn't going to get the chance to talk to her like he wanted to. He should have spoken to her while she was in the box with him. He should have tried to explain, made an effort, not let it come to this.

Now it was too late. The elevator was going to take him to the bottom, maybe past it into Hell itself, where he and the box would be engulfed in flames. He thought about the way everyone knew the elevator was old and unstable. When his body was discovered, everyone would think it had been an accident, chalk it up to the age of the building. They'd probably finally splurge for a new elevator to protect the other residents. Only he and Alice would know the truth of what happened to him, just as only he and Alice knew the truth of what happened to her. And Sunnycrest. The building knew, but it wouldn't tell, would it?

"Please!" he cried out to her. "I'm sorry! Alice, I'm so sorry. Please don't do this. Not yet. Please!"

The elevator stopped suddenly with another violent jerking motion. Huddled in the corner crying to himself as he waited for death to be upon him, Roger watched the doors working to slide open as slowly as ever. The metal moaned like it was in agony and then finally came apart.

Before him stood Mrs. Jackson, the African American lady that lived down the hall from him in Apartment 31. Seeing her brought back an entirely different trauma.

Roger was in his kitchen preparing dinner. He hadn't even met Lisa yet, but there was a beautiful girl he saw around the building he had his eye on. Her name was Felicia. Unfortunately, he didn't know much past that and he wasn't talented at breaking the ice and talking to new people. Most of his friends and girlfriends had been people his sister had introduced him to.

Still, he didn't want to fall into lazy bachelor mode. He made a conscious effort to stay away from a life of ramen and canned pasta and made himself cook real meals. If he ever got up the courage to talk to Felicia, he would invite her to dinner. He had music playing—grunge rock from his childhood—and he was wearing an apron, dancing about as he chopped vegetables.

There was a loud bang, a singular crack from down the hall that made him jump. The knife slipped and sliced through the side of his index finger. Roger cursed and quickly wrapped a towel around it. He was glad he wasn't attempting to entertain anyone.

The cut was shallow despite how much it bled so he just

washed it well, doused it in peroxide, and put a band-aid on. When he got back, he sighed with defeat upon seeing the blood all over his vegetables, so he decided to chalk this dinner up to a loss and order some Chinese food.

He cleaned up his mess as he waited for the delivery. Roger checked his phone when it buzzed to find an alert that his food was here, and the delivery man was on the way up. He grabbed some cash to tip the person and went to stand in the hall. When he opened his front door, he could hear a woman screaming.

Roger shivered and looked in the direction of the agonizing sounds. It was coming from Apartment 31. The Jacksons lived there. They were an older married couple whose kids were already grown and out on their own. Roger knew it had to be Mrs. Jackson screaming. He thought back to the loud crack he had heard earlier. Something terrible had happened and he knew he should help her somehow. He should, but he couldn't. He was frozen, petrified.

He watched Brian from across the hall fly from his apartment and run past his door toward the screaming woman. Roger stood there trying to remember how to breathe. He could hear Brian calling 9-1-1, saying something terrible happened and they needed help. Alice came out and asked her dad what was happening. He screamed at her to go back inside. Roger watched it all like it was a movie as he stood there nailed to his doorway.

The ding of the elevator drew his attention. He saw the delivery person exit into the hallway carrying his food. The person looked to his left and must have seen into Apartment 31's open door. He started murmuring and dropped Roger's food. Looking like he was going to be sick, the man stumbled back to the elevator.

Roger finally found his feet and took a single step into the hall to retrieve the bag of food the delivery man had left without being tipped. He grabbed the handles of the plastic outer bag and couldn't fight the temptation to turn his head.

Mrs. Jackson was on her knees sobbing into her hands. Brian rubbed her back. Mr. Jackson slumped on the couch—or at least what was left of him—the smoking gun still in his hands. Roger released the bag of food, no longer hungry, clamped a hand over his mouth and stepped back into his own place, closing the door.

22

ROGER HAD trouble looking at Mrs. Jackson without thinking about that moment and how he had failed to act, help, or do anything. He had heard the gunshot, the screams, seen the carnage, and he did nothing.

Then again, look what good it did for Alice when he *did* try to help. Mrs. Jackson was the one looking at him now, and her eyes definitely portrayed him as crazy. He didn't think she was wrong.

Word was, the Jacksons had been happy for many years, and it was a mystery as to why her husband took his life. The neighbors talked about Mrs. Jackson and made no effort to hide their murmurs. No one understood why she stayed at Sunnycrest or how she even could. The sight of her before him made Roger picture her on her hands and knees, rubber gloves up to her elbows, spraying bleach with one hand and scrubbing her husband's blood off the rug, couch, and wall. He remembered walking by her open door and averting his eyes, even when she was exhausted, sitting on that couch in the very spot her beloved died. She continued to sit on it to this day.

Now, Mrs. Jackson's face contorted, and her eyebrows raised as she looked down upon him, cowering in the back corner of the elevator. Roger still wasn't sure why it stopped, why it hadn't finished him. Was it simply because Mrs. Jackson had pressed the button? Did it stop for her? Why? Was this all part of the game?

"What's wrong with you, boy?" she asked him.

"N-nothing," he said, pulling himself to his feet and wiping at his eyes with the back of his hand, the gunshot firing in the back of his mind as he blinked away the memories of that grisly scene. "The elevator went a little crazy. Scared me, that's all."

It wasn't a lie. He just left out some major details, like the ghost that sent him back down the way he came.

Roger watched as the older woman shook her head at him. Frowning, he moved past her out of the elevator and into the lobby. He could hear Alice giggling somewhere off in the distance, impressed with herself for the prank she played on him. Judging by her expression, Mrs. Jackson didn't seem to hear the laughing child, so he said nothing.

Things were already awkward. So, Roger just gave the woman a forced smile and a wave. She didn't return the gesture. She stepped into the box and pressed the button for her floor, entirely fearless. Roger twitched. His instincts screamed at him to tell her to get out and not to trust it, but she already thought he had gone mad. Besides, he had left her to her own devices while she was screaming over her husband's dead body. Why save her now? He was no one's hero, not even his own.

As the elevator doors closed to take the woman home, Roger turned and headed toward the stairwell. He wasn't about to take another chance on the elevator. He doubted he ever would again. Roger fully intended to avoid all ways Sunnycrest could make him a permanent resident.

The door to the stairs had already been opened as if waiting for him, but it slammed closed as he reached for it, securing itself with a dull clicking. Roger stopped in his tracks and stared at the now closed door. He still felt like it was a safer option than the elevator. He had more control over his fate in the open space, and like it or not, he had to make it up one way or another. Still, Roger hesitated. He looked around the lobby to see if he was alone, or if the owner of the giggle that hung in the air lurked.

The only person Roger saw was Felicia, the beautiful red head from the second floor he still had yet to talk to. She was at the mailboxes with hers open, sorting through the contents. Lisa left him brokenhearted and lonely, but he couldn't bring himself to drag someone else into his world of madness. It was Alice's world now and that burden was his and his alone.

Roger often wondered what Felicia's story was. She could have easily been a model with her curvy shape, long legs, and wild, flowing, fiery red hair. The thick black glasses she always wore did not subtract from her beauty. In fact, in Roger's opinion, they added to it. They added a sweetness to her freckled, smiling face. Roger frowned at the sight of her.

"In another life," he said quietly, before returning his attention to the stairwell door.

Roger took a deep breath and grabbed the handle. Opening the door slowly, he peeked inside the darkness. No one moved up or down the stairs, but he was all too aware that didn't mean no one was there. He thought about how Alice had gone from standing beside him in the elevator to running past him outside of it in a blink. There didn't seem to be any rules to this.

Roger stayed as he was, listening for footsteps, breathing, talking, or that spine tingling giggle, some sign there was somebody in there waiting for him.

Everything was quiet, overly quiet. He could have heard a pin drop. It was the definition of silence, almost as if even the ordinary sounds had been negated somehow.

For a moment, Roger considered heading back to the elevator after all, but he thought better of it. He would be trapped in there. It was an awful feeling, being stuck and helpless. At least if something went down on the stairs, he could run, flee, make a case for escape. If nothing else, it gave him a chance to survive. That was better than nothing, which is exactly what the elevator had to offer.

He relented and finally entered the stairwell. Once he crossed the threshold, the door slammed shut behind him. He jumped, startled by the sudden noise, and grabbed the railing to brace himself, his heart pounding in his chest. He was so on edge. For a man who hadn't reached thirty yet, he felt in danger of a heart attack or a stroke if things kept up as they were. Then Alice wouldn't even need to take her revenge. With this in mind, he took several deep breaths to slow his heart before beginning his ascent. It didn't help that his mind went back to the day Alice died.

After catching the poor girl's leg in the door, Roger was afraid to run down the stairs. He knew he needed to hurry to keep from getting caught but was so afraid of dropping her. His eyes kept moving to her leg. It looked like it was definitely broken. He was glad she couldn't feel it. He was the only one feeling pain now.

His mind reeled, thinking about the parking garage and his neighbors and Brian, but he still moved with caution, trying with everything he had to keep Alice safe. The protector part of him hadn't shut off even after he had killed her. Did that make him good, or did it make him crazy?

Her eyes didn't offer any answer. They still looked panicked and wild. He tried not to look at them. Instead, he focused on the steps and making sure that he didn't miss any. When he opened the door on the second floor he stepped out of the stairwell and sighed, so glad to be away from somewhere that Alice could get further hurt.

23

NOW ROGER ENTERED the stairwell with empty arms, and it almost felt strange, like he was missing something, not protecting her as he should. "I'm sorry. I'll see you when I get to the apartment, I'm sure."

When he finally began making his way up the building's old stairs, each step creaked loudly under him, like the old metal bent under his weight, threatening collapse. Was it in danger of snapping? Was everything in this building on the verge of breaking and taking you with it? It was unusual for an apartment building to have metal stairs like these with a dangerous gap in between the flights. It made Roger wonder if maybe this building had been something else before it was an apartment complex. He didn't know much about the history of Sunnycrest.

It sounded like the souls of those lost to the building cried out to him for help. Maybe they were, but Roger had bad news for them. He was the wrong one to beckon to. He couldn't help anyone. His attempt to help Alice ended up feeding a new soul to the building. He had nothing to offer these spirits. He felt like he had nothing to offer anyone.

With another deep breath, Roger did his best to ignore the sounds and focus on making it to the seventh floor. *I just need to get home and put an end to this before it puts an end to me.*

As Roger made his way up the creaking, screaming steps, his paranoia drew his gaze to the next flight up, and then to the flight below in constant alternations. He had an overwhelming feeling he was not alone. Someone had left the stairwell door open for him and then slammed it in his face. Someone was in here. Even though he saw no one and the only sound was that of his own feet testing the limits of the steel steps, he couldn't shake the feeling. He thought back to when the maintenance man Tom had said at certain times of the year the stairwell was a bad place. He struggled to remember if that correlated to right now. He bit his lip as he tried to figure it out.

A terrible scream filled his ears then, cutting through the silence like a buzz saw and reverberating off the walls of the stairwell. It was the scream of a child. It didn't sound like Alice. He had heard her scream enough to know. The scream that rang down the stairs was blood curdling, full of anguish. It came from up high, higher than his floor, closer to the top.

Roger clenched his teeth and covered his ears, backing up until he could feel the wall behind him. Then the small body of a young girl fell past him toward the ground. His eyes widened in horror, and his mouth fell agape as he looked on in shock and disgust. That poor kid, there was no way she could have survived that, unless, like Alice, she was already dead.

Moving forward in a hurry, Roger peered over the railing. There was no small, crumpled body at the bottom. Then the scream returned. It was high pitched and ear piercing. Roger remained leaning over the edge, but he looked up in time to see the young girl come sailing toward him again, her face a mask of terrible pain. Roger moved at the last moment to avoid having her fall onto him, but it was enough for him to get a clear look at the child this time. He reached a hand out to try to grab her as she fell past him but his hand passed right through her as she sailed by.

Whoever the girl was, she had dirty blonde hair tied in two uneven pigtails and crystal blue eyes. She was wearing a yellow raincoat over a t-shirt emblazoned with a kids' cartoon character, blue jeans, and sneakers that had flickering lights on them. When he looked at the ground, she was gone again.

Roger didn't know who she was, but he knew she was dead, and he didn't want to know any more. Roger knew for certain now that Alice wasn't Sunnycrest's only spirit. How many more were there? How long had they roamed these halls? Terrified, Roger hurried up the stairs. He wanted to get to his apartment, to get inside and lock the door, even though he knew damned well it wouldn't do him any good. There was no such thing as locking out a ghost. Alice would come right in when she wanted to. Hopefully, she wouldn't bring this child with her. He remembered the ghostly voices of other children when he was trapped on the street and swallowed a lump in his throat.

As he rushed up the stairs, the child's terrible scream filled his ears again, echoing horribly in the acoustics of the stairwell. There was so much pain, so much sadness in the sound of it. He gritted his teeth against the feeling of the scream that leaked into his bones, but he kept moving. Shortly after the scream trailed off, the girl fell past him again, landing below with a sickening thump. Roger fought the urge to stop and look down again. Even after the sound of her small body hitting bottom, he knew he would see nothing if he checked. She would be gone from the concrete floor, ready to plummet again, reliving her final fall again and again. Tears filled his eyes for this child he didn't even know.

Roger groaned and bit down on his thumb. He had to keep going. The seventh floor was not much further. He was almost home. He started bounding and leaping up the stairs, two, three, sometimes even four at a time until he didn't land right, and his foot slipped. His face collided painfully with one of the steel steps and the jolt sent vibrations of shock through his bones. Curling onto his side, he moaned in pain.

Roger felt at his teeth to assure they were all intact. As far as he could tell they were, but his mouth was bleeding pretty good. Some of them did feel loose. He groaned, feeling stupid. Every time he attempted to flee, he ended up slowing himself down. It felt like someone had punched him in the nose as well, and unfortunately, he knew exactly what that felt like.

Twelve-year-old Roger looked out the third story window of his seventh-grade classroom. His sister was outside waiting for him. High school let out earlier than middle school. He was going to leave the window and rush down to meet her when he saw other kids from her school coming up from behind her. He felt a sudden sense of panic and worry. What did they want? They didn't look like friends of hers. He knew most of her friends and had crushes on a few.

The other kids surrounded her. They pushed her around. Roger's heart sank. He wasn't the confrontational type. He ran from everything, but his sister had always looked out for him. He couldn't just stand by and let her be bullied. Trembling with fear and adrenaline, Roger left the window and ran to the stairs. He charged down them at full speed, trying not to think about the fact he was running head on into danger. When he pushed that final door open and burst out into the sunlight and open air of the day, he saw them tugging on her backpack, shoving her, pulling her hair, and laughing at her.

Suddenly, anger replaced Roger's fear. He roared like the king of the jungle and charged toward the crowd of older children.

They weren't afraid of him in the least and went as far as to laugh at him as he ran at them. He still dove right in, his small fists swinging as he yelled at them to leave his big sister alone. His punches didn't seem to faze the older kids. They continued to laugh, then one of them grabbed him and held him while another threw a much bigger fist into his gut. Another fist hit his face. Before long, he was on the floor crying while being kicked by high top sneakers.

Roger had failed to protect his sister, but he succeeded in unlocking something inside her. The girl, who moments ago wouldn't fight to protect herself, unleashed on the bullies that were beating him up. She threw kids left and right, kicked them and punched them, dove on their backs and even headbutted someone. In moments, they all laid scattered about the school yard pavement, moaning and clutching injuries. Kara helped Roger up and smiled at him through tear-filled eyes.

"Thank you," she said, choked up. "I love you."

Roger smiled back with a brand-new gap in his teeth.

24

WITH HIS RIGHT HAND, Roger felt his eyes and cheeks to assess the extent of his injury. Everything felt okay aside from a little swelling, but his head was pounding. He needed to be more careful, or he really was going to be the death of himself, giving himself over to Sunnycrest. The ear-piercing scream rang out again, intensifying his already throbbing headache.

Roger pulled himself across the stairs to the railing. There, he looked up the stairwell. He could see the small blonde girl climbing the railing of the ninth floor, her pigtails swaying in a phantom breeze as she moved. *Why? Why would any child her age have a reason to take her own life?* He couldn't even imagine. Was she running from something?

The girl looked over her shoulder several times quickly, as if she expected to see someone behind her. Her face was panic stricken. She was terrified of something. Someone or something must have pursued her the day this first happened. Maybe they were chasing her, looking to hurt her, or they were already dead, and she was as frightened of them as he was of Alice. Could she have been haunted? Maybe the child hadn't meant to kill herself when she jumped, and she leaped over the railing in an attempt to get away from whoever or whatever was close behind. Or maybe, death was a better option than being caught. That was a terrifying thought, yet one he was close to understanding.

Roger realized he desperately needed some of his big sister's strength right now. He dug the phone out of his pocket and hit the button to call Kara while he watched the young ghost make the final decision and leap off, screaming as she went. He saw the sheer terror in her face as she fell past him and flinched hard when he heard her hit the bottom, despite knowing she was already dead and gone. The idea that the first time it happened she was there, broken, giving her blood to the concrete of the building, resonated with him, putting a terrible mental image in his mind, and leaving him nauseous.

Did that woman, Sarah, ever see this or anything like it? Would she still think him crazy or would she wish she had listened and left when he warned her to? He couldn't help but feel curious. He hadn't spoken to her since that first day despite the fact he did see her around occasionally. Maybe he should talk to her if he saw her again, if she was willing to talk to him.

Shaking his head, Roger forced himself to stand up, using the wall to brace himself on shaky legs as the phone rang against his ear. His heart sank when Kara's voicemail picked up inviting him to leave a message. What could he possibly say to explain all this in a thirty second message? With a sigh, Roger ended the call. He went to return the phone to his pocket when it slipped from his fingers.

"No."

Roger could do nothing but watch as it bounced off the step with a crunch that crushed the screen and fell all the way to the bottom where it exploded in a shower of plastic. He always knew he should get a protective case for it, but he didn't want to splurge and spend the extra few bucks. Now he had lost contact with the outside world. He looked at it down there, smashed on the first-floor landing and decided it wasn't worth going all the way down there to get it. He needed to finish going up, to face Alice. There was nothing to gain in retrieving his broken phone.

Roger felt dizzy and unsteady on his feet, so he took it slow this time. He ascended the last flight of stairs and sighed with relief when he reached the door marked seven. As he opened it, he could hear the girl screaming from above him again. Refusing to look, to see the death of the poor child one more time, Roger pulled the door open and started to exit the stairwell into the hallway of his floor.

He was stopped short as Alice ran past him again, her small black shoes clapping down loudly on the cracked marble tiles, giddy laughter emanating from her pale broken lips. Behind him he could hear the small girl's scream cut off abruptly as her body hit bottom again.

Roger shuddered. He found himself praying, something he hadn't done in many years, since his parents couldn't seem to decide on a religion and cycled through the options, changing their faith year to year. It wasn't a conscious decision. It was almost a reflex. His mouth started moving, and the words spilled out. Roger heard the words coming out of his own mouth, and it almost felt like he was listening to someone else. It was surreal and surprised him. Facing death was the surest way to find God, and Alice was death.

Before the small blonde could bellow her awful scream of stark raving terror and terrible anguish again, Roger stepped out into the hallway and let the door fall shut behind him, hoping it would be enough to keep him from hearing the terrible sounds of her looping death.

"Alice?" he said quietly at first. When he got no response, he repeated the girl's name louder this time. "Alice?"

Roger's head turned as he heard a nearby door opening. Mrs. Jackson stepped out into the hallway. Clearly, she hadn't had any problems with the elevator on her way up. At least he could feel relieved about that. He thanked whichever God he was praying to that she was safe.

"Boy? What is all the hollering about? You alright out here? Seems like something is troubling you today."

Blushing with embarrassment, Roger lowered his eyes to the floor. "Yes. No. Everything's fine," he told her. "I'm sorry for disturbing you."

"I think you're the one that's disturbed, honey," she said before going back inside and closing the door.

Frowning, Roger left the stairwell door at his back and headed toward his own apartment, the one marked 34, with the three hanging lopsided. As he fished around in his pocket for his keys, he couldn't help but wonder if the woman was right.

Roger hid in the closet with his back against the door, his thirteen-year-old face wet with fresh tears. On the other side of the door, his parents were arguing.

"Well, something is wrong with the boy, Fran!" He could hear his father bellow. "He's hiding in the damn closet like I'm the boogeyman. He's not right in the head. He's disturbed I'm telling you."

"*You're* disturbed, Tommy. As far as these kids are concerned, you *are* the damned boogeyman. Maybe if you would put that damn bottle down and get some help, your son wouldn't be hiding in the closet."

In the darkness of the closet, Roger hung his head, and balled his young hands into fists. "Just stop yelling," he whispered in the dark, over and over like a mantra. "Everyone just stop yelling."

25

AFTER ENGAGING the deadbolt and securing the chain on his door, Roger collapsed onto his knees. He made a feeble attempt to massage some of the tension from his bruised and swollen face. The bruise on the cheekbone below his left eye seemed to be getting worse. With a deep breath and a sigh, he tried to think of the best way to do what he needed to do. He decided it would be best to turn the TV on, to add some background noise and keep the conversation as private as possible. Even in Sunnycrest, he didn't want Mrs. Jackson and the others listening to him talk to the dead.

He just had to get up the strength to get up. He felt so exhausted after everything. He felt like he could stay right there forever, on the floor beside the door, like he could lay his head down and sleep on the cold ground. But he couldn't. He couldn't drag this on any longer.

With a groan, he pushed himself up, wobbling on shaky legs, a drum beating against his temples. He looked for the remote. Step one. When he finally located it on the glass coffee table, he snatched it up and pointed it at the TV, sitting down on the couch before he fell again.

Roger hesitated before pressing his thumb down on the power button. Reflected in the black glass of the blank screen was the image of the living room, warped by the rounded edges of the screen. Roger still had an old tube television his mother had given him. He had been meaning to get a new one, one of the flat screen plasma TVs that everyone else had, but he had never gotten around to it. It was never very high on his priority list.

Roger could see himself staring back in the reflection of the screen. He saw the couch he sat on and the end table beside it. He could see the lion print lamp a neighbor had given him when he first moved in resting beside a box of tissues on the end table. He saw the glass topped coffee table in front of him with a dessert-scented candle and a stack of magazines atop it.

Alice sat silently beside him in the reflection. She was resting with her legs tucked under her and her arms folded casually, looking back at him. She held that filthy old doll in her lap, one tiny hand on his knee and she looked like she had when she was alive.

Roger's eyes widened with the anxiety that she was already there with him. His lip quivered as fresh tears made their way to his eyes. He looked beside himself and sighed with disappointment to find an empty cushion. It was just like the elevator, and he couldn't understand why she chose to hide herself at times and not others. Why she went from looking like she did, to looking decayed and evil. He wished there was a rule book he could read.

Roger pushed the power button for the TV. With a click and a flash, the television came to life in front of him. He raised the volume to the point where it was loud, but not obnoxious. As much as he didn't want the neighbors overhearing the conversation to come, he didn't want them knocking on the door to demand he turn the racket down either. He wanted to assure that the next few moments were set aside for him and Alice only.

With the TV on and the volume up, he placed the remote gently back down on the coffee table. A line of sweat made its way down from his hairline, but Roger did his best to remain calm. Turning toward the cushion that appeared emptier than it was, he said, "Alice."

Roger paused for a moment though he was not sure why. Maybe he was hoping for a response or affirmation that she was listening, or maybe he just wasn't sure how to go about such a thing as this. It wasn't something people did every day, at least to his knowledge it wasn't. He knew there were people on TV who claimed to talk to ghosts on the regular, but he felt that most of that stuff was fiction.

After another deep breath, he continued, "There are no words to express how sorry I am. You have to know. You've been watching me. I know you have. I've seen you and heard you there. Haven't you seen my guilt, the pain I've been in? Part of me died with you that day. There is a piece of my heart and soul that will be gone forever. It left the moment I realized you weren't breathing and that it was my fault. I'm so terribly sorry. Do you believe me?"

Roger stopped again. How did he know if it was working? Would he just have to wait and see if she decided to leave him alone or kill him? That felt an awful lot like the life he was already living.

He sighed deeply, and told her, "I promise you it was an accident. I didn't know about your asthma. I swear. I didn't have any idea. I honestly didn't know. God, Alice, please forgive me. Please. I need you to know how sorry I am. Can you give me some kind of sign to let me know you hear me? That you understand?"

Roger could hear himself begging the child he couldn't even see, and tears welled up in his eyes. It made his swollen left eye sting, but he didn't even care.

"Please forgive me," he cried to her. "Oh God, Alice, please forgive me."

Catching movement out of the corner of his eye, Roger turned his head to face the television once more. The screen still displayed the syndicated sitcom that was showing when he first turned on the power, but over to the left of the screen, a television-like image flickered on and off in the air of his living room. The image of Alice warped and cracked with lines of static like a scrambled cable channel. It shimmered and twisted, blinking on and off in front of him. The sound of white noise generated by the distorted image of the girl he had killed overpowered the comic conversations of the television program.

Roger cringed as he stared into her flickering gaze. He was not sure if it was due to the presentation of it or not, but her guise was one of agonizing pain and torment. Her mouth was open wide and forming wordless screams of anguish. He watched as she appeared doubled over, twisted, and screaming, only to disappear and reappear leaning back and shaking with violent tremors, head bent up toward the ceiling. The slideshow of terror repeated itself and seemed to be endless, yet the only sound to reach his ears was that hiss and crackle of static, like a radio tuned into a channel with no station. He didn't know what to do. Was this her way of responding to him? How was he supposed to interpret it? What was she trying to tell him?

"I'm sorry!" Roger found himself screaming out.

Nothing else mattered now. Alice was everything. This was his chance to finally set things right. He needed to get through to her, to reach her somehow, to let her know how much this had eaten away at him, virtually destroying his own life. He needed her to understand he shared her pain. They were joined by it, tied to each other through it.

"What else can I do?" he yelled, the tears streaming their way toward his chin now, his swollen eye going bloodshot with the effort. "Please tell me what I can do. I'll do anything. I want to make this right, Alice. I just have no idea how. Please. If you can speak to me, tell me. I've heard your laughter, your voice saying my name. Do that again. Communicate. Tell me what I need to do to make things okay. I'm begging you. I need you to let me know you forgive me. Please. Speak to me!"

"It's too late," her voice said back.

The voice didn't come from her image. It traveled to him over his shoulder from behind the couch even as the constant recurring image flicked on and off before his eyes. The sound made him shiver and the hairs stood up on the back of his neck. How could she be before him and behind him at the same time?

Roger turned slowly to look over the back of the couch. As expected, he found nothing. Her voice and her image were in different places. Was that a sign of how fractured she was? Was that why she said it was too late? It was his fault she was like this. He deserved whatever was coming. He felt like his heart was breaking in his chest, splintering, and falling away piece by piece.

For a moment, Roger wished she would take her revenge and force him to whatever twisted realm she occupied. Maybe it wouldn't be so bad to be like her, to be a ghost. He wouldn't have to worry about bills and doing dishes. He wouldn't have to be so anxious and afraid anymore, would he? Would they be together? Or would he be isolated in his own earthly prison? Would it be painful? He knew he would somehow still be attached to this building. Just like Alice. Her body left, but her soul remained. He would belong to Sunnycrest like the blonde girl in the stairwell and however many others there were.

Roger wiped at his eyes and turned back around in his seat. The horribly flickering static image of Alice had disappeared and the TV was back to playing campy comedy as if nothing bizarre or supernatural had ever happened in the room. It looked like every other normal living room, only with a far less impressive television. Roger's breath escaped in a long sigh, and he slumped in his seat. He felt defeated. It was the only play he had, and it hadn't worked.

"It's too late," he repeated to himself, hanging his head. She was never going to forgive him. This was going to go on like this forever. She was never going to stop; never.

What did she want from him? What was her goal, her endgame? Did she want him to turn himself in, to admit the truth to the authorities and get her father pardoned? Was she intent on driving him mad? Did she want him to finally break and kill himself? Was it his life she wanted?

"Just tell me what you want! What do you want from me? What do you *want* from me?"

Roger couldn't bear to go on like this. Maybe that was what she wanted, for him to be tortured by her mere presence, and she already had it. It could be there was no cure, no fix, and it was something as simple as her trapped spirit wanting to see him suffer day in and day out. If she was trapped and suffering, it made sense she would want to share that experience with him.

Well, if that's the case, you got it, he thought. *You win. It's me and you. I sealed that the moment I took you into that laundry room.* "So, what now? Where do we go from here?"

Roger focused his attention on the show but found himself completely uninterested in it. Even if he was in the mood to laugh, the jokes were corny, and the laugh track made it almost unbearable. It was just another torture.

After what just happened with Alice, he wouldn't be interested in anything the box had to show him, but he needed to replace the thoughts racing through his mind with something, anything. The over-zealous family on the screen and the accompanying laugh track would have to do for now. If he let his mind dwell on the fact that the hope he had was pointless, resistance was futile, he would lose to it and succumb to his anxiety. "Is that what you want?"

When the show ended, Roger sat through another, but he always found his mind going back to Alice. He felt like he had literally fought to get home, struggled to survive her torment, and he did it on the hope he could make it back here and talk things through. It was all for nothing.

Would she let him return to work tomorrow? Would she come with him? What would that look like? He would call Mark if he had a damned phone, tell him what had happened, ask for advice.

It's too late.

That was all she said.

Did she mean too late for forgiveness? Did she want him to know, to live with that on his conscience? Did she mean it was too late for him to do anything to fix it? Maybe she meant that literally. Maybe he should visit Brian and ask him if he'd seen her, if he knew what she meant. Roger thought about the one time he went to see Brian behind bars.

Roger was having the worst anxiety attack of his life, but he needed to speak to Brian. He needed to know if he had been mistaken, if the articles and testimonies were right. He needed to know if Brian had been everything like his own father, or nothing.

He waited at the table alone, fidgeting nervously, hoping Brian would come out and grant him this talk. Part of him feared the man would see him and strangle him right there, not caring if the guards saw since he had already lost all that mattered. Roger pictured it in his mind, saw Alice's father killing him where he sat, over and over, until the man stood before him.

"You," Brian said, his eyes as dead as his daughter's were when Roger last saw her. "What else do you want from me?"

"The truth. I heard you scream," Roger said. He was shaking with fear. He felt like his heart was going to stop and he was going to die right there. "Day in and day out, I listened to you yell and stomp, hit the walls, and slam the doors. That isn't someone who is a concerned loving father."

Brian's eyes finally shone with light, the light of anger. He glared across the table at Roger. "And? You came here to condemn me some more? To tell me I was a failure as a parent?

My daughter is *dead*! Obviously I failed her!" The large man slammed a trembling hand down on the table. He was grabbed immediately and escorted away from Roger who sat there shaking.

"She had asthma!" Brian yelled, even as they told him to stop. "She refused to take her medicine or bring her inhaler. She was so obstinate, and her mother had already died during childbirth! I couldn't bear the thought of losing her too! And now look!"

"Enough!" a guard said forcibly. They were manhandling him roughly now, pushing and dragging him.

Brian would not be deterred. "You're right! You're all right! I was so scared for my little girl, for her health, so damned scared of losing her, that it made me crazy! Are you happy? Are you all happy?"

Roger couldn't speak. He just watched as the man was forcibly removed from the room as he screamed and wrestled against them, as he took their violence like he deserved it. Brian's words shook him to the core.

Could it be that he wasn't a monster? Was Roger the real monster? He was stunned and sat there in cold silence for several minutes before he could even begin to get up to leave.

26

ROGER WISHED Alice had said even a little bit more, elaborated on her thought. His mind was mush at this point. He couldn't figure out a mystery if it was the simple case of where he put his slippers when he took them off. She was the one who had gotten him here, scrambled, and unable to think clearly. She couldn't drive him to the edge of madness and then expect him to remember how to walk back.

Deciding he needed a drink, Roger pushed himself up from the couch and headed into the kitchen. His legs were shaky, and his balance was off. His nerves were completely shot. Opening the fridge, he reached in to select a beer, but cussed and drew his hand back. Closing the door, he reached up above the freezer instead, retrieving a bottle of whiskey. Beer wasn't going to do it—not when it was *too late*.

Twisting off the cap, Roger tossed it onto the counter and leaned back, turning the bottle up. After a few big swallows, he straightened up, grimacing at the burn in his chest. It was that feeling he had been waiting for, needing. The burn of whiskey traveled through him, warming and relaxing him. It always worked to lower his heart rate and relieve his anxiety. It wasn't the healthiest of cures, so he tended to only use it in emergencies, but he felt like that was exactly what this was. Now that he was coming down from the high of adrenaline-laced fear, he felt like he should wash up. The hot water would do him some good as well.

Taking the bottle with him, Roger walked through the bedroom into the attached bathroom. He wanted to take a shower, to clean up, to feel a little more like the one who was alive in this scenario—or at least look the part.

As he walked past the mirror over the sink, he looked at it cautiously, expecting to find Alice staring back at him. Only his own worn reflection resided there, and he sighed with relief.

Roger looked terrible. There were dark, sunken rings around his bloodshot eyes. His cheekbone under his left eye had already bruised, turning a mottled yellow and black, the swelling making it more prominent. He had wild stubble scattered across his face, and his lips were so dry and cracked they looked white. Dried blood crusted around his mouth, and he could still taste it swirling around his loosened teeth. His growing beard was sticky with old blood from his mouth and the front of his shirt was spattered with a blood and saliva mixture.

"I do look dead," he said to himself. *Maybe I am. Maybe this is hell, my penance for my sins.* He hoped not. If that were the case, then even death would not be an escape. He couldn't handle the thought of that, of this being his eternity. He could think of no greater punishment than living this torturous existence being stalked by his greatest mistake.

Frowning at his reflection, Roger finished the route to the shower, setting the liquor bottle on the floor nearby. Tearing the curtain back as if he expected someone to be standing behind it, he turned the hot water on. What did he expect to find? He didn't know anymore, but he knew he expected to find something. He always expected to find something, because so often something was there to find. That was how the day was going. It was what his life had become.

Closing his eyes, he took a deep breath of the quickly rising steam. He exhaled slowly and felt his nerves melt away. Then reality kicked him in the teeth harder than the steps had. He cussed and punched the wall. He hadn't gone anywhere to do his wash. He didn't want to put these bloody clothes back on. It was fitting though, an opportunity. Roger needed to get to the laundry room anyway. That's where it really began, not his apartment. Maybe going there would turn up better results, loosen the child's tongue. Thinking of it made his anxiety come roaring back.

Turning the water off, Roger closed the curtain, retrieved the whiskey bottle from the floor, and exited the room. On his way out, he didn't bother to look at the mirror, but he could have sworn he noticed Alice's image staring at him through the glass, palms against the fogged pane as if she were trapped within it somehow. Sadness shone in her emerald eyes as they followed him out of the room, but he never turned his head to meet her gaze.

"Soon," he said, punctuating it with a gulp of whiskey. "Why don't you just wait for me across the hall?"

Roger didn't drink often due to how it had affected his father. He definitely never drank liquor around Kara. She didn't care for it. He wasn't supposed to drink on his meds either. Neither reason stopped him now. He took another big gulp and shook his head like a wet dog attempting to dry off. Sometimes, he wondered if his dad had suffered from anxiety. Maybe the alcohol was his self-medication, but it only caused a whole other set of problems. Even after all these years, Roger tried to understand the man, what made him tick, what made him treat Roger and his family as he did. He never got any answers though, just more questions.

As Roger sat on the edge of the bed, he stared at the half empty fifth of whiskey and thought of the day his father died.

Roger was sixteen. He stared at the bottle in his father's hands because he couldn't look at the man's face. There was so much anger. His pale skin had reddened with it. There was a nerve twitching by his eye, veins that weren't ordinarily seen were bulging and pulsating in his forehead. His shimmering eyes were fixed on his son, fire burning in them.

"What did I do?" Roger asked sheepishly.

"You exist," Kara said angrily as she marched into the room. "He hates that we exist, that he screwed up and started a family. He hates that we cost money he could spend ruining his body with booze."

Roger flinched as the whiskey bottle soared past him and smacked into Kara's head. She cried out and hit the floor.

Roger finally turned his eyes onto his father, his own anger rising. "Get out," he said quietly but firmly. "I mean it. Go."

"She has no idea what the hell she's talking about," Roger's adrenaline-fueled father snarled.

"I don't care," Roger said. "Go."

"I love you. I love all of you," his father growled. "You have no idea what it's like. I'm in pain..." Roger's dad's thought trailed off. His face contorted like he *was* in pain, real physical pain. The anger changed to confusion, but his face reddened still. He grabbed his left arm and looked at Roger, his eyes pleading now.

Roger looked on in horror as his old man dropped to his knees and then fell onto his side, where he went still.

Roger was still there, staring at him in shock when his mother came in to look after Kara and take care of her wound.

Roger's eyes were pinned to the sightless eyes of his father when his mother said, "Good riddance. I knew it would happen eventually. I prayed for it. God finally answered."

27

THINKING OF HIS FATHER, Roger decided he had had enough to drink. He took a final gulp of liquor, then placed the bottle on top of his dresser. He felt depressed, lost, and alone. He walked unsteadily back to his bed, collapsing on top of it. It was still made. He didn't sleep in it anymore, not since Alice came back. Her return started with nightmares.

He got to the point where he knew sleep wasn't going to come, so he didn't even bother trying. Instead, he had become quite the regular at the 24-hour diner down the road. If they weren't open third shift and didn't offer unlimited coffee, he probably would have gone nuts a long time ago. It had been days since he had gotten proper sleep. Sleep was a privilege meant for ordinary people, people who weren't haunted, and Roger was haunted long before he met Alice.

When sleep forced its way to him, and it always did eventually, it was usually on the couch with the nearby television playing as a distraction. Even then, it was short-lived. The nightmares would always come. Roger had been plagued by nightmares most of his life.

Teenaged Roger awoke covered in sweat and fresh tears, a scream still clinging to his lips. Kara was beside him. She held tightly to his clammy hand. "He's gone, Rodge. He can't hurt us anymore. It was just a dream."

It wasn't *just* a dream though. It was a nightmare. It was horrifying. Even now that he was awake, he could still see his father clear as day behind his eyes, screaming and glaring. He shivered and hugged himself as the vision of his father breaking the bottle in his hand for a better weapon and marching toward him intent on murder, refused to fade.

Kara climbed onto the bed and hugged him. "I have them too, you know. It's okay. They won't last forever. It's just going to take time. It'll get better."

"Yeah," Roger said quietly, the image of his father striking down upon him with the sharp serrated edge of the broken glass, playing in his mind.

28

BETWEEN PURE EXHAUSTION AND WHISKEY, it didn't take long for sleep to find him today. It took even less time for the nightmares to find him, for Alice to find him. The dreams were different this time. They weren't full of ghostly, violent images of her. She didn't chase him and laugh at his fear. She didn't attack or eat him.

It was that day all over again, the day it had all began. He saw it again, felt it again. Alice's tiny form, so afraid of her father, then so still in his arms. It was a disease that fed upon him. He had been reliving his nightmare via his subconscious for a long time, long before Alice had come to visit, but once she had, the reality left and made way for far more terrible things. This was the first time in a while he went back to it, his darkest truth. He saw her as she was, an innocent child, a victim.

He awoke crying atop his made bed, clammy with cold sweat and feeling the need for that shower more than ever. Images of the laundry room down the hall remained, imprinted on his mind. It was like his dream was setting the mood, getting him prepared for what he had to do next.

He sighed. He slammed his head into the mattress. He hated himself. He despised who he was. He wished he could have been a smidgeon of the person Kara was. She wouldn't have been afraid of Alice's father. She would have known exactly what to do. She still would, if he would open up and talk to her, but he hated bringing his baggage to her. Kara had bailed him out and taken care of him his entire life. It wasn't fair to her. She deserved good things, the life she worked hard to earn, not to just be his eternal caretaker. He warred with himself, going between bringing Kara in on his curse and cutting ties with her completely to save *her* for a change.

Try the laundry room first, he told himself.

What if he subjected himself to the torture of going to the laundry room only to find out once again it was too late?

Maybe it was a side effect of the whiskey, but he found tears rising in his eyes again. It was not the fear of Alice being there, full of hate and vengeance, that was eating at him. It was the idea of going there and being forced to confront his own demons, to remember the awful thing he had done, to relive it all over again. It was one thing to relive it in his dreams, but to do it awake was a different story.

He knew. It would all come flooding back at once the moment he entered, but maybe that's what needed to happen.

Roger shook off the spell the whiskey had on him and wiped at his eyes. He did so a little too aggressively without thinking and pain flared up in his swollen cheek. He grimaced and grunted, touching it lightly with his fingertips. It felt so strange, so large and unnatural, so much like that day the bullies handed his ass to him.

Roger glanced over at the piles of his filthy clothes all over the floor. He sighed and headed back to the kitchen where he opened a cabinet under the sink and retrieved a couple of large lawn and leaf trash bags with the intent of filling them with his dirty laundry. He let the cabinet doors swing shut behind him as he turned away. Before he took his first step back toward the bedroom, he could hear the cabinet door swing back open behind him. Roger shook his head and rolled his eyes. He didn't care for any more games.

With a sudden blast, his faucet came to life behind him, furiously spraying water.

Roger's heart jumped and he growled in frustration. "What is the point of this? Why don't you just talk to me and tell me what you want from me, what you need?"

"That isn't me."

Alice's voice came from before him. Roger lowered his gaze to see the girl standing beside the couch, staring at him, a wicked smile curling her decaying blue lips. Roger gasped but he tried to reel in his shock. Maybe she was ready to talk.

"See you in a bit," she said before running right through the front door like it wasn't there. He watched her disappear and sighed.

"Alright," he said, struggling for a deep breath. "Okay."

Behind him, a quick tug pulled the cabinet door shut. The bang of the slamming door was enough to give Roger a start. His heart pounded again, thundering inside him. When would it finally give out on him like his father's had?

Roger heard the sound of something falling in his bedroom. The bang and jingle of shattering glass made him wince. He sighed his frustration.

"Was that my ghost or someone else's?" he grumbled. "I'm beginning to hate this building."

Trash bags in hand, he made his way back to the bedroom.

The first thing Roger did when he crossed over into the bedroom was search for the fallen object. There was a framed photo of him and Lisa together at the park lying face down on the rug. He frowned. He wasn't sure why he had kept the photo when it was a reminder of what he had lost and seeing it only served to keep his pain fresh, but he couldn't bring himself to get rid of it.

Maybe he needed to hold on to hope, or maybe it was more simply that he needed to keep the evidence of a time when things were better, to remember that it wasn't always like this. Maybe seeing proof of that single memory tethered him to sanity and he was afraid if he let it go, that cord would snap. It might already be too late.

Either way, the picture had been all the way back on his dresser against the wall. There was no way it could have fallen that far on its own. Had it been Alice or whoever had been in the kitchen harassing him? He thought of the little girl in the stairwell, and it turned his stomach. The whiskey threatened to come up. He knew Alice wasn't the only ghost in this building, but he needed for her to be *his* only ghost. He couldn't deal with another. The thought of it was too much for him to handle. He considered giving up right then and there, just laying down on the ground where he was and waiting for whatever came.

Roger dropped the trash bags to the floor and bent down to grab the picture. When he stood with it in hand, he lingered and stared at it for a moment. He really was happy back then. It was written all over his face, in his genuine smile and relaxed posture, and, if he had to bet on it, he would have said Lisa had been happy too. There was love in her starry-eyed gaze and gleaming smile. There was a time when he really believed they were going to end up getting married. Maybe they would have if it hadn't been for Alice and her father.

Sighing, Roger stood the picture back up on the dresser where it had been. If it was Alice, what was her message to him in breaking it? Was she trying to show him how she would shatter his happiness? Maybe another ghost was trying to make him look at it and remember the good. He didn't know what to think.

He grabbed the first trash bag, and he stuffed dirty clothes in it, grabbing handfuls at a time from the floor. He needed to act fast before he lost what little nerve he had left. It wasn't much to start with, not when it came to Alice. He didn't want to end up taking his clothes down to the laundry room on the first floor where he would wash them, change, and leave. It wouldn't be a stretch for him to leave his bags of clothes in the laundry room when the front door and freedom were so close by. Though it would be running away again, and that never solved anything.

Roger rubbed his bruised face. He stopped what he was

doing when his eyes found their way to his bed. It was swollen like someone had lain in it, the sheets and blankets raised in a human form. Tracing their path up to the pillow, his eyes found it to be indented with the small shape of a child's head. Roger hadn't slept under those covers for some time, but somebody else had. How many times? How often was she there, in his bed, sleeping on his pillow? Was she there at the same time as him, lying next to him?

He pictured the image in his mind and gasped. He saw himself laying in the bed and Alice's corpse curled up behind him, a blue-tinted arm wrapped over his midsection. The thought alone made him feel more nauseous than he already did. He was beginning to think the whiskey had been a really bad idea. It had certainly been a bad idea for his father but that never seemed to stop him either.

Roger covered his mouth with his hand to keep the bile down. He remembered covering Alice's mouth with the same hand. It was so innocent a gesture. How could he have known it would lead to her death? He had wanted to keep her quiet, to save her from being hurt, not to...

Breaking free of his trance, Roger yanked the covers down. There was nothing there to see but the sheets that lined the mattress. Looking back at the pillow, he discovered it had puffed back out to normal. He closed his eyes and took a deep breath. It wasn't real. Maybe none of it was real. He saw what she wanted him to see.

Shaking his head, Roger opened his eyes once more. When he did, he caught a brief glimpse of color within the bundle of sheets he had just pulled back. Curiously, he reached out. With trembling fingers, he grabbed the blanket and moved it aside. A toy doll tumbled to the mattress and landed on its back staring up at him. It was filthy and obviously old, and he knew it well. The right leg was missing below the knee. That part was new. It was a silent way of reprimanding him for what had happened to her leg as he carried her out of here.

"At least you didn't have to feel it," he said. Roger shook his head and chastised himself for his insensitivity. It wasn't like him, and it wasn't going to win her over. Maybe part of him wished she would kill him. Maybe he subconsciously wanted to anger her.

Roger reached down and scooped the doll up, holding it before him. There was no denying the doll in his hand. It was as real as he was. Roger watched the doll intently, waiting for it to speak or attack, to curse him accusingly, but it did no such thing. It just laid there, limply within his grasp as dolls did and stared back at him through hard plastic eyes. Even her doll was accusing him.

Roger wanted to toss the damn thing out the window, but he felt like he had to respect it, to treat it with care. It was an extension of the child. Frowning, he tossed it gently onto the mattress.

"Here," he said. "I'm sorry about her leg...and my rude comment. Why don't you take her back though? You can probably take better care of her than I could. I'll just leave her right here for you, okay?"

He looked at his palms. After holding the retched doll, he felt filthy himself and was overcome by the need to wash his hands, to remove the germs of the dead from his flesh. It was a good chance to leave the room for a moment and allow Alice to collect her doll. He walked carefully to the bathroom and scrubbed his hands vigorously, glancing over his shoulder at the doll on the bed. Roger took a deep breath and stared at the mess he was in the mirror. He took some water into his palms and splashed it upon his weary face.

When he glanced at the bed again, the doll was gone. He found himself smiling at this. Had he actually done something right? He turned the water off and headed back toward the bedroom.

He grabbed the bottle of whiskey from the dresser for a few more sips—bad idea or not—before retrieving the garbage bag.

Since he was lacking in God-given bravery, maybe some liquid courage would help him along. It was worth a try.

After already feeling queasy, it probably wasn't the best plan to continue drinking. He figured if nothing else, he might just get drunk and be less aware of what was going on around him. Maybe he would even pass out and get that much needed rest he could never seem to attain. At this moment, intoxication certainly didn't seem too bad, though he was pretty sure one good encounter with Alice would sober him up in an instant.

Terror was sobering. Fear and terror were different things. He had been anxious and afraid most of his life. He had never known true terror until recently. That thought made him feel the need for another drink. It was a vicious cycle.

"Like father like son, huh, Dad? When are you gonna come pay me a visit? You could show up randomly and just scream at me like the good old days."

After another few good sips of whiskey had his head swimming, Roger went about finishing the task of stuffing the first bag full and pulling the drawstrings tight. He hurriedly grabbed the second bag and started to fill it with his clothes when he heard the sound of rustling plastic beside him.

Roger glanced over to see what was happening now. His eyes went wide when they fell upon the trash bag he had just finished loading clothes into. The drawstring handles were now tied in a secure knot, and it looked like there was a small person trapped inside the bag, trying their damnedest to fight their way out.

The plastic jutted out this way and that, as hands and feet pushed against it from the inside. He could hear the muffled sound of someone struggling for air within the bag, moaning and gasping.

Roger remembered Alice suffocating in his arms, the way she had coughed and choked. He felt a sudden surge of panic. Maybe she was giving him a second chance to save her. Could this be his chance to redeem himself, to earn her forgiveness? There couldn't be much oxygen in that tightly sealed plastic prison, and the poor kid had asthma. He remembered the inhaler he had stepped on and broken earlier, and he frowned. If Alice were having an attack inside that bag, she would die all over again. Was that even possible? Could you die twice? Maybe not ordinarily, but he wouldn't put it past the laws of Sunnycrest. He pictured the girl jumping off the stairwell in his mind.

Roger dove into action, grabbing the bag as it squirmed and moved about the floor at his bedside. Hands and legs pushed against the plastic but were unable to break through. Roger dug his own fingers into the plastic and tried to rip it apart so he could free the child within.

"I'm trying," he said. "Save your air. Don't die on me. I'm trying. Come on!"

It was hard to help her when the bag constantly moved, legs kicking furiously from within. It was flopping everywhere.

"Hold still!" he called to her. "Please. I'm trying to help you. Just relax. I'll get you out. I promise."

She must be so scared, he thought.

Finally, he felt his index finger punch through the plastic, and he worked to stretch the hole. At least that would let some air in. It could be enough to keep her on this side of life. Maybe she still had a chance. He could do it right this time. Roger could actually save her, rewriting both of their fates.

He tore at the bag wildly with both hands, until the bag finally split apart. Roger's clothes spilled out all over the bedroom floor. *What the hell? No!*

Alice was nowhere to be found. Roger gripped the bag tightly in his hands and bowed his head, closing his eyes. Tears leaked out from under his closed lids. He thought he was going to be able to do what he hadn't done the first time and save her, but it just had been more proof he couldn't. What was done was done.

When he opened his eyes, Roger threw the shredded bag onto the ground. He could hear what sounded like several children, all laughing at him. Roger nodded angrily. "Laugh it up."

Roger thought about going to get another bag from the kitchen, but he quickly remembered the cabinet and what had happened, and he decided against it. One would just have to do for now. This wasn't really about the laundry anyway.

Roger grabbed handfuls of the clothes now scattered on the floor before him, and he stuffed them into the remaining bag. He left the rest on the floor, deciding he would pick them up later. He wanted to get to the laundry room before the effects of the alcohol wore off.

Roger pulled the drawstring tight and stood. He eyed the whiskey bottle and considered more, but he already felt a little off balance and thought he probably shouldn't overdo it. He didn't know what was going to happen once he got to the laundry room. He didn't want to think or feel, but he wanted to be able to run if he needed to. He found safety in running.

Carrying the overstuffed bag with him, Roger headed to the front door of the apartment. He set the bag down but hesitated, pausing before the door. Alcohol or not, he didn't feel strong enough to do this, but he knew there was no choice, no other way. As he stood there, the chain undid itself and fell away from the lock. Roger stared at it dangling there before him. Swallowing hard, he watched as the deadbolt disengaged without his assistance. Alice must want him to enter, or someone in this building did at least. They made the decision for him.

He clutched the doorknob with a shaking hand. Closing his eyes tightly, he did his best to regain composure, considering the alcohol again. But he knew if he turned back to the bedroom, he wouldn't go at all. He needed to press on, to stay on course.

"Alright. Let's go," he said to Alice, trusting she could hear him.

Tearing the door open, he grabbed the bag of clothes and stepped into the hall. He stopped in his tracks when he caught movement out of the corner of his eye. Turning slowly, he saw Alice's dad entering his old apartment and shutting the door behind him, but that was impossible. The man was in prison, where he had been for months. Had they released him? Was it possible he had gotten free, and Roger had not heard about it? Could he have gotten out for good behavior or something like that? Roger had seen those things happen on TV and in movies. This was not good. It was not good at all.

Roger stood in the hall, watching the door, and waiting for the man to come back through. Even after he discovered Brian wasn't the abuser he had thought him to be, Roger did not fear him any less. He was still big, loud, and intimidating, a clone of Roger's own father. He also remembered the man's anger from the last time Roger saw him. If he was back now, Roger doubted the man would have been humbled by the prison sentence. More likely, it was the opposite, and he was probably full of hatred and brewing for vengeance of his own. Roger's heart pounded in his chest as the moments passed by, but the door never moved.

Maybe it wasn't Alice he was supposed to face. Maybe this was the answer. Suddenly, Roger wished he had brought the remaining liquor with him. Closing his eyes, he took a deep breath and went to Apartment 33. He lifted his hand to knock.

"It's now or never," he told himself. "Let's get this over with."

29

AFTER ROGER KNOCKED on the door, he couldn't breathe. The anticipation of waiting for it to be opened was painful. When it finally did, he jumped before seeing who was on the other side.

The twenty-something female that stood before him looked sweaty and dressed for yoga. "Can I help you?" she asked.

Roger blinked. He was still shaking from his nerves. His mouth was dry. He licked at his lips, struggling to wet them. "I, um, I'm sorry. I thought I saw a man walk in here, a man that used to live here. I guess I was mistaken."

"Well, that's more than a little creepy. Judging by the fact that you look downright terrified, I'm assuming he wasn't a very nice man."

Roger swallowed a lump in his throat. "Depends on who you ask, I guess."

"I'm asking you."

Roger nodded. "Yeah. Then pretty bad I guess, but obviously he's not here, so I'll let you get back to it."

"It?"

Roger bit his lip and shrugged. "Exercising or whatever. I don't know. I'm sorry."

"You're a bit weird, buddy. You know, I've lived across from you for over a month and this is the first time you've spoken to me."

"Over a month?" Roger looked confused. That didn't seem right to him. Was he so lost in his own problems he hadn't noticed someone move in? Maybe they were on different schedules.

"Yup. A month last week. I'm Rebecca. And you are?"

"A jerk, apparently," Roger said with a smile. "My name's Roger, and I'm really sorry."

Rebecca smiled back. "Well, I'm gonna get back to exercising or whatever, as you put it. It was nice to finally meet you, Roger. I figure you can't be too bad. Your daughter seems to really love you. She follows you around like she's your shadow."

Roger's eyes widened. He swallowed nervously. "Thanks," was all he managed to say.

He watched in fear as his neighbor waved and closed the door. Then he looked around for Alice. He was alone in the hallway. He put a hand to his mouth as a shiver ran through him. Rebecca had lived there for an entire month, and he had just seen Brian walk right in.

Was he hallucinating? He frowned, trying to figure out what to do.

His gaze moved to the door to the laundry room. He was so afraid of it now. He was afraid it wouldn't just be Alice who came to him there. But how could he walk away without at least trying? He couldn't keep going on like this. If it didn't go well, he deserved whatever he got.

That's what he told himself as he took a deep breath and left Alice's old apartment to head to the place where she died, the place where he killed her.

Roger was uncomfortable being in a funeral home. He hadn't

been in many. The whole atmosphere made him feel uneasy. It felt worse knowing that his father was laying in the casket. His mother hadn't wanted to come to this, but Kara said she needed to see him dead, to know that he was really gone. Now Roger was here, and he didn't know what to think or feel. He was scared and he wasn't even sure why. His father had been the scariest thing in his life, and he was gone. Maybe it was his body here in the room that frightened him?

Roger swallowed a lump in his throat and walked down the aisle toward the waiting casket. He felt a little sorry for his father that there were so few people here. He knew how his father was, but he felt like everyone should have someone to care about the loss of them. He hoped in his young heart that he would have people when he passed away.

Though it will probably just be Kara, he thought.

Then in his mind, he pictured her standing alone in an empty funeral home with him in a casket nearby. When he came back to reality, Roger frowned. At least it was a normal reaction given the circumstances and no one would look at him like he was strange.

When Roger reached the casket, his breath seized. His father's eyes were closed, and he looked peaceful, but being this close to him after the rage that had fueled him right before his death still left Roger afraid.

Part of him was honestly sad. He wasn't sad that this man was gone. He was grieving for what he never had, for the father he never got to have. Now his father was dead and there would be no changing, no reconciliation. It felt heavy in his chest.

He felt someone beside him then and Roger turned to see his mother standing there.

"He got what he deserved," she said matter-of-factly. "It was his own evil that took him. He was fueled by the drink and the drink came back to get him. It's what's right. Don't shed a tear for that man." Then she turned and walked away.

Roger found himself feeling real sorrow for the man in the box. Kara came up and took the spot beside him. She gently rubbed his back. Roger laid his head on her shoulder.

30

WHEN ROGER ENTERED the laundry room, it looked exactly as he remembered and how he saw it in his nightmares. Already, the anxiety crept in like a silent assassin. Thoughts of his father's funeral were still fresh in his mind.

A row of three washers on the left and three dryers on the right lined the walls of the small room, with just enough space between the rows for a single file line of people to stand. The back wall displayed a box that dispensed powdered soap and fabric softener when the appropriate change was inserted. Below the box was a small blue wastebasket. One dim light bulb hung overhead swinging rhythmically back and forth.

There was nothing welcoming about this room even for people who had not suffered a personal tragedy within its walls. It was even worse for Roger. He tried to remain focused.

Start your laundry, he coaxed himself onward. *Do what you came here for. Let's go.*

Roger set the garbage bag down and rubbed his sweating palms together in an effort to dry them. His breathing was labored as his nervousness took hold.

Bending over, Roger opened the bag, when he heard coughing and wheezing sounds coming from in front of him.

"Is that you, Alice?" he asked. "Are you here?"

Reaching into the bag, Roger pulled forth a large handful of clothes. Behind him, back in the hallway, he could hear a door open and quickly slam shut. The sound was followed by that of young feet tramping quickly down the hall. He didn't need anyone to tell him which apartment it was. But how could she have been coughing before him and just now running from her home? So many times, she seemed to be in two places at once. Maybe there were more children here. He imagined them hanging together, roaming the halls.

"Do you have friends here? I'm glad you have company at least. Death always seemed so lonely to me."

"I'm not here," a voice whispered into his ear. "I'm out there."

Roger looked at the door. His heart was beating so hard, it felt like it was going to burst out of his chest onto the floor of the tiny room. In his mind, he pictured just that, and saw himself staring at the organ still pumping blood at his feet.

Roger worked to breathe slowly and steadily to calm himself. As he did this, he approached the door. He cracked it open and peeked into the hall, wondering if Rebecca would see or hear him and think him even crazier than she probably already did. He didn't see any sign of Rebecca or Brian who, if his eyes hadn't deceived him, were both in Apartment 33. He did, however, see Alice standing nearby, fear and anger on her face, pink cheeks wet with tears that continued to spill from those beautiful green eyes. She looked as he remembered her, before she started coming to him in her decrepit ghostly guise. She looked like the living, breathing Alice, the real and true Alice, the Alice he had murdered.

What would she have been if he hadn't tried to save her? It was something he often wondered, what he stole not just from her, but from the world. He couldn't think about that now. Now was his chance to set things right. Maybe that was why Brian was there. The moment had to be complete. He felt like he was no longer in the right now with Rebecca in her new residence. He was in the past. He was reliving the worst day of his life. He couldn't focus on that though, because if he did, he would miss his chance to change it, to set it right. Damn his anxious mind. He left the laundry room and knelt before the frightened child.

"I know you're scared, but I won't let him hurt you," he said to her. "You've got to believe me, Alice. I won't let you down this time. I promise."

Alice stared back toward her own apartment. Roger knew there would only be a few moments before that door opened and her enraged father came bounding out, sick with worry, whether Rebecca was inside exercising or not. They were living two different days simultaneously. Somehow, it made sense to him now. He knew he wasn't crazy. This was real. All of it.

Instinct told Roger to grab Alice and take her into the laundry room, to keep her safe but he knew that was the wrong course of action. He had made that mistake once already. He would never forget the outcome of it as long as he lived. This time, he couldn't run. He had to do what he was never able to do with his own father. He had to do what he did for Kara at school that day. He had to stand up and take his beating.

Maybe it wouldn't even come. He remembered what Brian had said to him that day at the prison. He was just frightened. He loved her. Maybe he could be reasoned with. Maybe Roger could even get Alice to understand her father's intentions and not be so afraid. He took a big, deep breath and gently moved Alice behind him, standing between her and the door to Apart-ment 33. Then he turned back around to face her. He felt anxious with his back to that door, but he wanted to get Alice into a position of security before talking to her.

"It's okay. You're safe."

Alice's green eyes roamed his face for a brief moment but then returned to the door to her home.

"Alice. Alice, can you hear me? I won't screw this up, not this time. Okay? You're gonna be alright, sweetie. Trust me."

Alice turned to face him at last, lingering there, but she looked nervously at the door to her own apartment. He noticed the similarity in her body language and facial expression to the blonde girl who took the swan dive in the stairwell. What had she been so afraid of? She must have had her own monster chasing her.

Focus, Roger! He's coming.

Roger took a deep breath. It felt like it was caught in his chest. Air was hard to get, damned anxiety. "Alice, honey," Roger said, his voice quivering. "I know your father seems mean, but he loves you. You know that, right?"

The little girl looked at him with her big emerald eyes and nodded her head.

"Okay," Roger said. "Well, the reason he wants you to take your medicine is because it's very important. I know you hate it. I hate taking medicine too, but when you don't take medicine, bad things happen. Your dad just wants you to be okay. He wants to keep you safe. So do I."

She stared hard at him with those big eyes of hers. Her look intensified as the green faded away. A blackness spread until her eyes were completely gone and only darkness remained.

"I'm already dead," Alice said.

Before Roger could say anything else, she was gone. "No. No, no, no. Come on. Come back. Please!" *Please.*

Roger saw Brian come flying out of Apartment 33, sailing through the closed door—probably unbeknownst to Rebecca in downward dog. Still frightened of Brian's wrath, Roger ducked back into the laundry room and eased the door shut so it closed with a quiet click.

He trembled terribly and his leg started its usual panicked shaking, foot tapping the floor. He feared the sound of his tapping foot would give him away, so he did his best to force it still, grabbing it with his hand. Then the sound of phantom coughing entered the room with him. He looked and Alice wasn't there, not visually, but her asthma remained.

Through the closed door, he could hear Alice's father screaming her name, his voice full of panic and fear. Roger thought it still sounded like anger and rage to him. Could one lead to the other?

When Roger had spoken to Alice, she had known she was dead. What was done was already done. That didn't mean Brian knew he was dead though. What would he do to Roger if he found him? The coughing grew louder as if Alice knew he was intent on staying quiet and worked to sabotage his efforts. He looked down. This time Alice was there, looking like she had the day he took her life. She coughed and choked, a hand to her chest.

Roger was not going to try to stop her cough, not this time. He knew better. He would never forget what happened when he tried to stop that cough; a child paid with her life. Instead, he could save her, bring her to her father, get her medicine into her. He knelt and scooped her up into his arms, eyes on the door.

He was doing what he should have the first time and how it ended would be how it was supposed to end. It was not history repeating itself as it usually did but correcting itself for a change. He struggled to stand without dropping her or hurting her in any way. He would never forget about the poor girl's leg.

When Roger got the door open, he found himself face to face with Alice's father.

The man dove in closer, pointing his finger at Roger and screaming, his face red as a beet, spittle flying from his mouth as he bellowed the word, "You!"

Instinctively, Roger backed up. "I know you're angry, but she needs you. She's sick and needs help. Please."

Before he realized it, he was pressed against the wall, the cold metal of the soap dispenser box on the back of his head. Alice's father rushed toward him, his face flushed red with rage. Roger turned his head to the side and squeezed his eyes shut tight. He could smell the man's sweat and sour breath, both of which sang of alcohol. Behind his eyelids, Roger saw his own father there, ready to beat him, bottle in hand.

"I'm sorry," Roger cried.

He expected to be pummeled or torn apart, but it never happened. Time ticked by silently aside from the pounding of his terrified heart. Roger was afraid to open his eyes.

Below him, his foot started going, tapping away erratically. He had already been found, so there was no reason for him to try to control it or curb it. He just let it go. Roger could still feel the man's hot breath on his face.

"You're just like your goddamned mother," his father's voice said.

Suddenly, Roger found himself wishing he was still trapped with Brian. When he finally opened his eyes, he discovered he was. Alice's father stood before him in an orange jumpsuit. He stared at the wheezing girl in Roger's arms, pointing at her paling face.

"Just like your hard-headed, stubborn ass mother," he growled.

"What are you talking about?" Roger snapped. "She's sick. You can save her. She needs her medication. Take her home!"

"We *are* home," Brian said to him, a thin stream of spittle hanging from his lower lip.

Roger trembled but there was nowhere to run, and Kara wasn't there to save him. For once in his life, he had no choice but to stand his ground. "Save her!"

"Like you did?" Then a door slammed in the hallway again and Roger jumped. When he looked again, Brian was gone.

"Why?" he cried. "Why wouldn't you save her? You're the good guy. I'm the bad guy. You're supposed to save her!"

Roger looked at his arms and found Alice was gone too. Maybe her father had actually taken her? He didn't believe it though. Then again, he didn't know what he believed anymore. He'd seen his own father and he wasn't even part of this story. Nothing made sense.

Pushing himself off the wall, Roger fumbled in his pocket for quarters. Roger knew the drier could calm his anxiety. He was trembling so bad he was waiting for his heart to give out at any moment.

His eyes fell on the bag of clothes, and he sighed heavily. He still needed to do his laundry. With shaking hands, he dropped the quarters in the box, and quickly pushed the button to dispense the laundry soap. Roger wanted to get the washer going and focus on the spin and rumble to calm his heart. He hurriedly dumped the bag of clothes inside.

Roger waited impatiently, foot tapping away, for the box of detergent to drop down into the tray below. When it landed where it should, he snatched it up immediately and turned to the open washer. With his nervous unsteady fingers, he worked to pry open the corner of the detergent box, spilling some of the powder in the process.

When he finally completed the simple task that seemed unreasonably difficult, Roger leaned over the washer and his mouth fell open. His hand released the box it was holding, and it fell, hitting the floor and spilling its contents everywhere but into the machine it had been meant for. Inside the washer with his clothes was something else. A pale limp arm protruded from the pile of shirts and pants, the hand hanging loosely to the side, one nail missing.

Alice!

Surrendering to instinct again, Roger dug through the clothing in an effort to unbury the small child. Inside, he knew she was already dead. She had said it to him herself. But for some reason, just as he had back at the apartment, just as he had when he put her in the car the day it all happened, he couldn't shake the feeling he needed to help her. Tearing at the clothes, Roger yanked them out of the machine, tossing them over his shoulder onto the powder-covered floor.

When the girl's still form was finally uncovered, she didn't look to be breathing. His heart sank. She looked so fragile, so pale, just as he regretfully remembered. His heart broke at the sight, cracking open like a coconut to expose the pain at its center.

Scooping her out of the washing machine, Roger held her, unmoving, in his arms, just as he had before he ran that day. This poor, sweet child was so cold to the touch, so very cold. Roger held her tighter in an effort to warm her but checked to make sure she would be able to breathe this time.

Roger stood there cradling Alice in his arms and rocking her like a baby, telling her to wake up and breathe, but she did not. She laid like a doll, like her doll that had fallen from her grip. It wasn't here now, but he could see it behind his eyes. Alice's plastic-looking eyes were frozen open and staring nowhere. Alice was already dead.

"I'm already dead."

He could hear her saying it again in his mind. Roger felt himself starting to cry. He quietly apologized to her, as he had so, so many times before. He brushed the hair out of her frozen face.

Roger's head cocked to the left as the door came open once more. It didn't fly open as it had with the intrusion of the dead girl's enraged father. Instead, it popped open with a gentle click. A man in a custodian's jumpsuit entered, his gaze on the spilled powder and wet clothes all over the floor.

"I hope you plan on cleanin' this mess up," Tom said pointing at the detergent and scattered clothing. "I swear you people think because I get paid to clean this place that means you can make all the damn mess you want. That's a load of crap."

"I...I'll take care of it, Tom," Roger told him. "I'm sorry. It was an accident."

"Yeah, you will take care of it," Tom said back with a huff of irritation. "You plan on washing those clothes or just standin' there and huggin' em like your childhood teddy bear?"

Roger looked down to find his arms full of nothing but laundry, his own soggy, dirty laundry. He took a long, slow, deep breath, then shook his head and let the pile fall from his hands to join the rest on the floor. The powder seemed to respond, swirling around the room. Roger grimaced, realizing Tom glared at him. Roger immediately scooped the clothes back up and tossed them in the washer with a barely audible apology.

As Roger fished out more quarters for a new box of soap, Tom huffed and looked at the ground, watching the powder fall back to the floor. Instead of spraying everywhere like it had been, it landed in neatly piled clumps that seemed to form letters. Roger stood there with his new box of soap, watching as Tom squatted down with his dustpan and hand brush.

"Well, will you look at that," Tom said.

Roger's eyes took in the powdered detergent and the letters they had formed on the ground. They spelled out the word, *Sorry*.

"That you, Eddie?" Tom questioned. "I knew you were here somewhere. That's why I ain't quit this God awful place yet."

Then he used his small hand broom to shovel the letters into the dustpan. "The dead never leave this place," he said.

Roger said nothing. He figured the word was meant for him, not Tom, but he didn't want to debate it. Somehow, he thought it didn't have anything to do with Alice either.

Me too, he thought. *I'm sorry too.*

Then Roger just poured the powder over his clothes, closed the lid, and started the washer.

"I'm sorry," Roger's father said as he drove.

From the passenger seat, Roger just sat silently, staring out the windshield with fearful eyes. He could smell the alcohol on his father's breath. It filled the already stale air of the car and his young nostrils. Not only did the sour odor make him feel sick, but it scared him because of what it represented. Roger knew that drinking and driving was bad. It was dangerous and got people killed. In his mind, he pictured the car wrecking in all different ways, tumbling and rolling, crashing into other cars, plowing through a guard rail. In each vision, he died a horrible death.

"I had to take you because your bitch of a mother won't let me see you. You understand, right?"

Roger was still thinking about dying in an automobile accident.

"Son. Answer me. You understand, right?"

Roger came back to the real world and looked over at the drunken driver. He shook his head. "No. You've been drinking. You shouldn't be driving," he said, voicing his anxiety.

"And you shouldn't be telling me what to damn do. I'm the parent."

Sirens sounded behind them, and his father cursed. Roger sighed with relief. In his head, a vision of their tumbling car came to a halt. Roger's fears changed then. He pictured his father getting out of the car and yelling at the police. He saw them raise their guns. Everyone was screaming and then Roger was screaming too as his father was gunned down.

When the vision ended. Roger looked at his father with worried eyes. He put his small hand on his father's much larger one that gripped the gear shift.

"It's okay. I understand," Roger said quietly. "Don't argue with the policemen. Please."

The car came to a stop, and Roger's father put it in park. He sighed and looked over at his son. "Sorry, kiddo. I just wanted to take you to the park and have some time with you. I'm sorry it's like this. I'm sorry for everything."

That was the first time Roger had ever heard his father apologize where it sounded like he meant it. He couldn't help but smile.

31

BACK INSIDE HIS APARTMENT, Roger leaned against the closed door and covered his face with his hands. He couldn't take much more of this. He had already leaped over his limit as far as he was concerned. He needed to figure out how to end it, but he had no clue where to begin. He couldn't give her what she wanted because he didn't know what she wanted. Why wouldn't she just tell him?

Sighing, Roger headed through the house to locate the liquor bottle. Tonight, he would drink until he forgot and tomorrow, he would go back to work and see what happened. There was no way to guess the future in such a predicament. All he could do was hope for the best, and even that seemed far-fetched at this point.

Knowing good and well that Alice might be cozy in his bed waiting for him, Roger didn't want to sleep there. She had been next to him on the couch too. He didn't want to be in this apartment at all, or even in this building. With an exasperated sigh, he took a big gulp from the liquor bottle. At this point, he didn't notice the burn anymore. It might as well have been water.

"Is that how it was for you, Dad?"

Roger took another sip from the bottle and almost choked as something solid floated into his mouth and to the back of his throat. Coughing and gagging, Roger doubled over. He could feel the item fall from his mouth to the floor in front of him. He coughed some more, confused and disgusted.

"What the hell?" he aid out loud to no one in particular, his voice filled with shock and dismay.

Panting heavily, he looked down onto the floor to see what had gotten into his liquor. On the floor at his feet was the dirt-stained head of the same doll he had found in his bed earlier this evening, Alice's doll. His stomach turned and he felt like he was going to be sick.

Cupping his hand over his mouth, Roger ran for the bath-room. He dropped to his knees, throwing the toilet seat up in a single motion. When he found the body of the doll floating in the water of his toilet, he turned his head as a reaction and vomited onto the bathroom floor. He cussed, but he couldn't stop it. It just kept coming. He was heaving, releasing all the alcohol he had taken in.

Roger slumped to the floor, tears streaming down his cheeks. His guts twisted into knots. His head spun and he thought alcohol might not have been the best idea after all. He felt posi-tively awful. He wiped at his mouth with the back of his hand. "At least I hurt myself and not other people when I'm drunk, right, Dad? You sorry bastard."

Roger looked up to see his father standing over him. "You didn't have to get drunk to hurt someone, did you, boy?"

"I guess not, Dad. Sorry, Alice. This is my dad. He's mean like yours. Difference is my dad almost never meant well."

A few more dry heaves racked Roger's body. He panted and gasped. When Roger regained his composure, he used the toilet to brace himself and get back to his feet. Doing his best not to step in the pile of sickness on the floor, Roger made his way toward the kitchen. His stomach still didn't feel right, but he knew it would pass. It wasn't the first time he had drank until he got sick. He wasn't proud of it, but that didn't make it any less true. There was a lot he wasn't proud of, Alice topping that list.

Roger decided it was time to go see Kara. It was a safe place outside of this building. He wished he could call her first, but it wasn't an option. Hopefully, she wouldn't mind the intrusion. He felt confident she would be able to help him. She had never judged him before; mothered him yes, but never judged him. Maybe she could get him some help, take him to the hospital, call Mark. Kara and Mark were the only people he trusted anymore. He started the day, trying Mark. Now it was time to try Kara. That was about the extent of his resources.

Leaving his bathroom a mess like the rest of his place, Roger grabbed his coat and headed out into the hall. Instinctively he searched for any sign of danger, but the halls were as lonely and quiet as a cemetery. The only sound was the rhythmic turning of the washing machine behind the closed door of the laundry room. Roger hurried away, running past the laundry room to the elevator.

It didn't take Roger long to get to his sister's place. That was one of the perks of Sunnycrest. It was close. He knocked on the door, trying not to seem too frantic and activate her worry button.

The door opened inward, and Kara invited her brother in with a smile. Roger thanked her and walked past her to take a seat on the couch. While she disappeared into the kitchen, Roger was antsy, shifting in his seat. He didn't know if Alice had followed him as she had when he went to see Mark. The last thing he wanted to do was drag his sister into his mess and sick his ghost on her.

Roger hoped Alice would allow him a brief respite from her harassment. He didn't see her on the way over to his sister's as he had expected to. He had been anxious the whole way, searching the shadows and listening to every sound the city night offered him.

Instead of being relieved, her absence left him on edge, panic constricting his chest. He felt like it had been too long, like it was the calm before the storm. It was mental warfare, part of his punishment.

Kara returned with a plate of pasta and a fork. "Eat," she told him. "It looks like you haven't been. You need to get some nourishment. I really need you to take better care of yourself, Rodge. You worry me sick."

Roger frowned, but he knew better than to argue with his big sister. He nodded and accepted the plate. The food tasted divine, even to his angry stomach. Mid-bite, he said, "Alice is back."

Kara frowned. She sat down on the couch with him, setting her own plate on the coffee table. "I knew it was the anniversary of when all that happened," she said. "Finding a dead child like you did, carrying her all the way to the hospital...that would mess up anyone. But you have to know she's never coming back. She's gone. You can't bring her back. No one can, and not to be insensitive, but please don't get any sauce on my couch."

Roger shook his head and put his plate down on the coffee table beside hers.

"You're wrong," he said. "Ghosts are real, Kara, and Alice has come back. I've seen her and heard her. She's here, Kara. She's here and she's angry and she's making me crazy. She's never going to let me go."

Kara sighed. She eyed her little brother with sympathetic brown eyes. "Eat," she said, gesturing at the food on the table before him. She waited until he picked the plate back up. Only then did she pick up her own.

"Grief does that," she told him. "You're not the first person to see and hear a dead person they had trouble letting go of. It's really natural. You're not being haunted. I need you to trust me on that. I wouldn't lie to you. I'm on your side, always. You know that."

"But you're wrong this time," Roger said.

He ate some food and then gestured at the plate with a thumbs up, as he wiped at his mouth with a napkin. "I've seen her father too, and he's not even dead. Maybe I'm just cracking up, Kara."

Kara's face made Roger put the plate down again. "What is it?"

"He *is* dead Roger. He just died. Suicide, they think. Don't you watch the news?"

Roger's eyes widened and he shook off a chill. "He came right to me," he said. After a deep breath, he laid down his empty plate. "Kara, I also saw Dad...our dad."

Kara looked taken aback then. She looked away from him. "Why now? I thought the nightmares stopped years ago."

Roger slowly shook his head. "I think it's the building, where I live... it's like a gateway."

Kara reached over and grabbed her brother's shoulder, giving it a supportive squeeze.

"Look. Stay here for a bit then. You're safe here and we can find you someplace else to go. Okay?"

Roger considered her words. It did sound like a much better option than going home to Alice and the others. He felt safe for the first time since Alice had returned. Kara was always his safe place.

"Only if you keep cooking like this," he said, discovering he still knew how to smile. He honestly couldn't remember the last time he had before that moment.

"Definitely," she smiled back. "I seem to forget I live alone when I cook, and I always end up with enough leftovers to feed the city's homeless for a week."

"Well, I'm not homeless. I'm just haunted." He gave another smile, but it came out a little awkward and not as genuine as the last.

Kara got up and padded into the kitchen where she fixed herself a glass of wine. She brought an empty glass back with it, along with the bottle.

"Merlot? You know, Rodge, if there was any place in the world I believe could be haunted, it would be Sunnycrest. I had my own experience there once when I was visiting you. I didn't tell you because it felt crazy." She shivered to prove her point.

"Tell me now," Roger said. "It'll be good to hear about someone else's experience, to know it isn't just me. Please."

Kara sighed and nodded. She raised her glass. "It was when you had gone back home to visit Mom and asked me to stop by and water your plants."

Kara closed her brother's apartment door and locked it with the spare key he had given her for emergencies. She walked to the elevator, checking her watch to see how many steps she had taken in visiting her brother's seventh floor apartment. She would have gotten all her steps for the week if he had lived on the thirteenth floor, but she was still ahead of the game as far as her goal of 100,000 for the week.

She could have added to it by taking the stairs like she had on the way up, but she felt like she deserved the rest. She was only on her lunch break and had to get back to work. She didn't want to wear herself out too much.

When the elevator arrived, she got in and hit the button for the lobby. The box jumped and rumbled, and it made her put a hand to her heart. She wished they would fix things around here. Then there was a banging on the roof like someone had jumped onto it. The whole car shook under the weight of whatever it was.

Kara stared up, waiting for something else to happen. Then the elevator stopped, and behind her, the doors struggled to open. When they did, she turned around and stepped out, but she couldn't resist a look over her shoulder. What she saw made her shiver again. A man stood in the elevator, right where she had been standing. He stared up at the roof just as she had been.

"Oh no, Kathy, no," he said tearfully. Then he turned to Kara and stared at her through tear-filled eyes. "She jumped. She jumped, and it's my fault."

Kara didn't know what to do, or what to think, but if someone really jumped, then she needed to get help. She looked toward the front entrance and then glanced back at the open elevator to find the man was gone. Kara stood there for a moment trying her best to put together what had just happened, but she couldn't. She shook her head and hurried out of the building, down the walkway and the street.

32

ROGER SIGHED. "THAT'S TERRIBLE," he said after hearing Kara's story. "If the man in the elevator was the ghost, then what if Kathy had actually jumped and was on the roof of that car?"

"I checked the papers for days, looking for an article about someone ending up dead there or at least an obit for someone named Kathy, but I never saw anything. I thought I must have been crazy, overworked and stressed, or something. Well, drink some wine. Relax." Kara smiled at him in her motherly way. "After we find out who is getting kicked off American Idol, you can get some real sleep. A shower probably wouldn't hurt either."

Roger accepted the offer and poured himself a glass.

"You gonna tuck me in?" he asked.

"Do you need me to?" Kara said with a chuckle.

"No." Roger laughed. Then his face got serious. "Maybe."

"I'll do it," she said, turning on the television. "You know I'll do it."

They shared a laugh and the rest of the wine. They watched the show together and even though it wasn't something that interested him, he had a good time just being normal, just being her brother. It was a nice change of pace. He was glad he came to her. It was proving to be exactly what he needed, but something in his gut knew it was temporary.

It was also comical to Roger just how much his sister cared about the strangers on the TV. She yelled and clapped and even cried a time or two when she didn't know them any more than she did the people that passed her on the street. Kara was a character for sure.

When all was said and done, exhaustion was definitely getting the better of him, and the warmth and security of her house took him over the finish line. Kara did in fact tuck him in before turning off the television and retiring to her bedroom.

For the first time in what felt like forever, Roger slept soundly. Nothing woke him. There were no ghosts, crashes, creepy noises, or feelings of someone touching him. He did dream of Alice, but it wasn't a terrifying nightmare. Instead, he dreamed of her in a sparkling white hallway. Her doll was clean and whole and brand new. She smiled and reached toward him. Her lips moved, but he couldn't hear any words. It felt peaceful.

When he woke up in the morning, he wondered if maybe she had forgiven him and moved on to Heaven. She could have come to him in a dream to tell him, couldn't she? He could only hope.

Roger felt going to Kara's had definitely been the right thing to do. He should have done it a long time ago. He'd always known that Kara would take care of him. He just didn't want to trouble her. He felt like such a burden when it came to his sister, even if she had told him a thousand times never to feel that way.

Awake and feeling good, Roger made his way to the kitchen for breakfast. There was a note from Kara on the door to the refrigerator. It listed possible breakfast options and their locations so he could fix them for himself. She must have already left for her own job.

Roger glanced at the clock on the microwave and saw it was already the middle of the afternoon. He blinked and rubbed his eyes. He had really crashed hard. He had it coming. He had needed the sleep, but now work was out of the question, again. He had already missed most of his shift. Truthfully, he wasn't sure he still had a job. Maybe if he had made his sales quota they wouldn't mind his coming and going, but his leads proved fruitless and his numbers were bad. That was enough for him to get fired without even missing any work.

Maybe it was time for him to find a new job. He hated that place anyway. It wasn't paying the bills as it was. Today was the first. His rent was due, and he was a few hundred short. That was one thing he definitely didn't want to ask his sister for help with. He needed to be adult enough to pay his own bills. Kara did enough.

He would have to go back to Sunnycrest to give old Agatha what he had when she came to collect, even if he did plan on moving. He couldn't just skip out on rent. He had done enough wrong. He was anxious about going back, but at least he would know how much truth there was to his dream. Maybe when he got back, he would find Alice was finally gone. He prayed to anyone listening that would be the truth.

Roger found a piece of paper and a pen and left his sister a note thanking her for her hospitality. He wondered if he was actually free, or if he had just learned how far Alice could reach. Couldn't he have just gone past the length of her leash, tying her to the building? He would find out soon enough.

Not wanting to rush back home on the chance he was completely wrong about Alice and this small slice of freedom was the only one he'd get, Roger stopped for a pretzel and a soda. He sat on a bench to enjoy them after smothering the pretzel in yellow mustard.

Roger realized then someone was saying something to him. He turned to look and see who and found there was a strange young man with a ball cap and a hooded sweatshirt staring at him, his eyes aloof and overly dilated.

"Alice said to come back home," this young man said. It reminded him of the way Lisa had broken up with him. Could someone be playing a prank on him? It was an awfully mean thing to do if they were. He had been outside Sunnycrest when that happened. Had Alice seen? Maybe she was making him relive that on purpose. Did that mean she hadn't forgiven him after all? He didn't want to jump to conclusions. Maybe he hadn't even heard the boy correctly.

"What did you just say?"

The young man became more alert. He rolled his eyes.

"Man, Alice says you need to get your ass back home. She needs to talk to you."

Suddenly the pretzel felt dry and unpleasant. Roger choked on it and quickly took a gulp of his soda. He hoped this was the conversation he'd been waiting for, that she was going to tell him it was all over, that they were good. He threw his remaining pretzel to a group of nearby pigeons and tossed his soda can into a recycling bin. Then he took a deep breath and stood. Sunnycrest was waiting. It was time to go pay his dues.

When Roger got back to Sunnycrest, the front door to the building was open again, the screaming mouth of the brick face ready to consume him. It was as if the building expected his return, telling him to go on and go inside. Wind whipped at the big tree and a familiar colorful plastic ball bounced out the front door and rolled to a stop at his feet. Roger found himself trembling, suddenly afraid. The sight of the beckoning building made Roger want to run. He was through running though. Running and hiding were what had gotten him into this mess.

He stood before the towering beast, his leg tapping nervously. "I'm coming."

Roger took a deep breath to steady his frayed nerves, though he couldn't stop the trembling and his anxiously tapping foot. Before he could change his mind, Roger marched almost confidently into the mouth of the beast called Sunnycrest. As soon as he did, the mouth shut behind him with the sound of a slamming door, swallowing him into its depths.

An old woman came out of an apartment on the first floor as soon as he was secured inside.

"I thought that was you," she said.

Roger wanted to ask why, to tell her he didn't know her, and she had no reason to be expecting him. Then he saw her bend down and smile at the empty air before her. She hadn't been talking to him after all. She was talking to someone or something only she could see. She was probably a victim of Sunnycrest just like he was, just like they all were. The building sank its teeth into everyone.

Instead of feeling more frightened, Roger felt energized by this. It made him angry, and anger propelled him. For someone with such terrible anxiety, anger was one of the only motivating forces he had. He didn't want to waste it. It was the only thing his father ever gave him.

Roger went to the elevator and aggressively pressed the up button. He didn't care if Alice rode with him this time or if she sent him flying back down. He would take the ride, wherever it took him.

"Let's go," he told her.

It seemed to take forever for the steel death trap to arrive. When at last the creaking, old doors jarred open loudly, Tom the custodian stepped out. He gave Roger an irritated look and then walked past him without so much as a word. Roger frowned and raised a hand in a half-assed wave.

He got into the elevator and hit the button for the seventh floor. The elevator smelled strongly of bleach. It burned his eyes. Tom must have been cleaning it. Was the mess what had the man upset? Roger wondered what had happened to dirty the inside of the elevator so that it required bleach. He couldn't help but remember Kara's story and looked up at the roof.

When the doors opened, Roger stepped out into the hallway and looked both directions for any sign of danger. Alice didn't go running by this time. The hall was eerily quiet as it had been when he left. It added to the feeling that the building was waiting for him, that Alice was waiting for him. He felt like he was doing exactly what he was supposed to do. This was his fate. He had sealed it a year ago. He felt surprisingly calm and accepting about the possibility of it ending with his death. He was glad to have spent time with Kara in case it was.

Roger paid a visit to the laundry room before going to his apartment. No one was around but the washer stood open. Roger took a peek inside. He would need to rewash his clothes since they never got dried. They'd be mildewy after all this time. It was a waste of quarters but the least of his problems.

The washer, however, was empty. Roger scrunched his face thoughtfully and inspected the driers on the other side. Sure enough, his clothes were in one. Someone had finished his laundry for him. Was it Tom? Maybe Mrs. Jackson had done it for him. Maybe it was Alice giving him an olive branch.

"Thank you, whoever you are," he said loudly.

Roger left the laundry room and hurried to his front door. He needed a new bag to retrieve his clothes. The numbers on his door had been fixed, screws tightened. That must have been something else Tom had done for him. Tom was cryptic and grouchy but all in all, he was a good guy.

As soon as he crossed his threshold, Roger locked the door immediately out of habit. He ran his hands through his knotted, unbrushed hair, and rubbed at his stubble-covered face. He went to the kitchen for a garbage bag to put his clean clothes in. Then he made his way back to the living room.

"Alright. I'm here," he said. "I came home, Alice. Now what?"

There was no response. Roger huffed and unlocked the door, heading back into the hall, not looking over his shoulder for once. There was no point.

Roger went to the laundry room and started putting his clothes into the bag. "Having the guy give me your message was a nice touch. But you wanted me here, and I'm here, and you're not saying anything. I don't understand."

With the bag full of clothes hoisted over his shoulder, he walked back to his apartment. "Talk to me," he said, no longer caring who heard him. "How about you, Brian? Dad?"

When Roger was back inside, he dropped his clothes on the floor by the door. "Alright. Well, I'm gonna have some coffee then. I'll make some extra in case your dad or my dad wants some. But you'd probably prefer a different kind of drink, wouldn't you, Dad? It's in the bedroom. Get it yourself."

Roger headed for the kitchen where he made good on what he said. He even went as far as to pour a second cup which he sat on the kitchen table in front of an empty chair.

"There you go. So, how long are we going to do this?" he asked. "When are you going to open up and talk to me?"

There were still no words or sounds from Alice, but her father made an appearance. He stood next to Roger, towering over him. The man truly was massive. He bent over to stare into Roger's face, but Roger didn't turn his way. He stared forward at the empty chair and continued to sip at his coffee, even as the man got so close he was almost touching him, and Roger could feel static electricity jumping off of him.

"Your cup is over there," Roger said, pointing. Moment after moment passed by and the dead man continued to stare directly into Roger's face from centimeters away.

When Roger finished his coffee, he set it down on the table and stood from his seat, still without looking at Alice's father, who moved to follow him and maintain his hard stare. Roger felt proud of himself. Brian wasn't any less intimidating, but Roger was handling it, holding his own for once. He wasn't going to budge no matter how afraid he felt. This was what he needed to do. He needed to be strong for once in his life.

"Well, if you're not going to have it, I'm gonna drink yours too," Roger said to the staring ghost without directly looking at him. His daughter still hadn't shown up to the party.

Roger walked around the table and picked up the other cup of coffee he had set out. He took a big gulp and then coughed and choked, splashing coffee on himself. Roger cussed and dropped the cup onto the floor where it shattered. Then he spit the dirty plastic doll head onto the floor amongst the glass. Apparently, Alice hadn't been as absent as he'd thought.

"I hate that doll," he said, wiping his mouth. "I hate that frigging doll. I know you love it, but I don't. Please stop giving it to me."

He looked at the broken coffee cup on the floor and the new addition to the mess that was his apartment and he sighed. He really needed to get this place cleaned up, but he just couldn't bring himself to do it. Even the thought of it felt entirely over-whelming.

"Hey, Dad," he said. "Since you're here. Why don't you clean that up for me? Make yourself useful, huh?"

Roger's attention was drawn to a knock at the front door. He hoped it wasn't Kara. She had work today. He would hate for her to screw up her job because of his mess. He screwed up his own job. He didn't need to extend that courtesy to her. He didn't want to interfere with her life any more than he already had. Enough was enough. She deserved a better, stronger brother than the one she got.

When he reached the door, Roger stared through the peep-hole before doing anything. Through the hole, Roger could see old lady Agatha standing impatiently on the other side. She was there for the rent.

Well here goes, he thought.

Agatha came to Sunnycrest every month and dealt with all of the occupants, and she always seemed uncomfortable to do so. Surely, there was a good chance she would believe in the super-natural and the spirits that haunted this old building. Maybe he could just tell her he didn't have the rent in full because he was haunted.

Roger sighed and gave in to his conscience. Opening the door, he put on his best smile and said, "Agatha, good to see you."

Roger stepped out into the hall to meet the small, frail-looking woman. He didn't want to let her in and have her see the mess of his apartment.

"I'm sorry it's a little short this month, Agatha. I'll have the rest for you soon," he said with another exaggerated, crazy-looking smile.

Roger noticed the old woman's gaze wasn't cast upon him. She watched something else or someone else. Was it Alice? Old Agatha had always seemed haunted to him, even before he knew the truth about this place. Roger wondered if people now said that about him. Did they notice how troubled and absent he was? How distracted? Was it visible to the outside world?

"You okay?" he asked her.

He watched as she broke away from whatever she was looking at and listening to and turned to face him.

"I cannot stay long," she said to him. "I just need your money, Roger. Then I'll be on my way. Just give me what you have so I can get out of this building."

"Right," Roger said, scratching at the back of his neck. He dug in his pocket and pulled out his wallet. He retrieved a folded envelop from behind his business cards. "Here ya go," he said, handing it to her.

Agatha looked at him for several seconds without saying anything. Then, at last, she blinked and sighed. "Okay," she said. "Call me with an exact date and an exact amount."

"I will," Roger said, forcing another smile. "I'm sorry to be so much trouble, Agatha."

Agatha didn't seem to be listening anymore. She wasn't even looking at him. The small, hunched over, old woman focused beside him. Roger stood there awkwardly, waiting for her to return to reality. Seconds ticked by and the silence became unbearable. Roger's anxiety kicked in and his foot got to its usual tapping.

It felt like time froze, like he was the only one moving in a still snapshot of the world. It made Roger want to scream, but he didn't dare. He kept his frustration internal and stayed where he was, simply watching and waiting. What was Agatha even doing? Did she see Alice?

Finally, after what felt to Roger like an eternity, the old

woman broke away from whatever spell had her so entranced. She took a deep breath and let out a long exhale that carried the weight of heavy emotion and then she turned back to Roger, blinking her eyes.

"It's okay," she said.

Roger awkwardly smiled at her. "Alright then, Agatha. Thank you for being so understanding."

Agatha nodded at him, then turned and headed for the next apartment when she paused. She turned and said, "It's not my place, but that young girl is suffering. You are making her very sad, and she wants you to stop doing this."

"Doing what?" Roger asked, but Agatha immediately moved over to the next door and knocked on it. There was nothing to stop him from following her, from asking what she meant, but the old woman didn't seem eager to elaborate, so he went back inside.

"How come after everything, you will talk to old lady Agatha, and you won't talk to me?" he said when he entered. "Are you even there? I can't see you. What has changed, Alice? Tell me. Tell me what to stop doing."

Again, silence was the only response he received. Roger huffed.

He waited. He listened intently. Nothing.

Roger sighed. He opted to go back to the bedroom. He climbed into bed with his hopelessness and wrapped himself in blankets. Then he drifted into oblivion. There were more knocks at the door, but he slept through them all.

Roger slept through the following day. His body had reached its limit and refused to give in any longer. It was demanding rest, taking it by force. Depression overpowered him. Stress had finally taken its toll. Roger couldn't find the energy to get out of his bed. Even when he woke up, it was short lived, and he would just fall back into restless slumber.

When he finally dragged himself out of bed, Roger had no

idea how long he'd been in there. His body was stiff and sore, and he smelled of stale sweat.

Roger stumbled from the bedroom. The world swayed and tilted. Everything was blurry. He went to the filthy bathroom that stunk horribly of his own stale sickness and urinated. His head was pounding. When was the last time he took his meds? He couldn't remember. He felt so confused. Was this Alice's doing? Sunnycrest's?

He needed coffee. He'd just slept too long. It would be alright.

Roger's head hurt something awful. Where was Alice? Where was her dad? Were they still there with him? Were they just watching, hiding somewhere? He wouldn't have been surprised to hear them laughing at how disoriented he was, reveling in his pain.

Roger couldn't see or hear either ghost. He could barely see or hear anything. How long had he been asleep? How long had it really been since he had left Kara's house? He told her he would stay with her. She would be worried. He should call her. Where was his phone? He couldn't remember. It was all a blur.

Roger's memory was as fogged as his actual vision. His head pounded like a bass drum. His heart raced, but it sounded erratic. Was it his ears or his heart? He was holding onto the door to his bedroom and swaying with it.

Back and forth.

Back and forth.

Roger could hear someone calling his name. It was a voice he knew, a voice he recognized but he couldn't place it at first. Then it became clear to him.

It was Alice. Finally.

She was finally ready to talk. Roger had no idea how long he had waited, but she was finally calling him. She sounded like she was in the living room. Her voice was loud, panicked. She sounded alarmed and afraid. Maybe it was anger. Was she angry?

Would he be walking directly into a punishment? He couldn't tell.

"I'm here," he said back. "I'm in here. I'm coming out."

Roger stumbled out of the bedroom, and he saw the front door standing wide open. He remembered locking it. How was this possible? Who had opened it? How long ago? Where were they now? Was he being robbed?

Alice continued to call for him. "Roger! Roger!"

His nervous eyes scanned the apartment, but he didn't see an intruder. Had Alice opened the door? Why would she need to use the door? Something wasn't right. "Is someone else here with us?" he asked.

"No, it's just us," Alice said back to him. "It's just us now. Me and you."

"What do you want me to stop doing? Tell me what you want!" he yelled.

Alice's voice spoke back at him, "I want you to come with me and leave this place."

Roger saw her then. She was coming in from the kitchen. She was marching toward him with a confident swagger. Her black dress matching her hair began to blow in a breeze that affected nothing else around her.

Alice's black shoes clapped the floor like some evil tap dance routine as she approached him. He still felt so dizzy, but he knew he had to get away. He thought he could accept death, allow her to take him, but he couldn't. He wasn't ready.

"I'm sorry," he said to her. "How many times do I have to say I'm sorry? I never meant for this to happen."

"You don't have to be sorry. Just come with me."

Roger hurried around the coffee table, stumbling, and almost going down. He looked over the couch and saw Alice still marching toward him, her face a mask of anger and hatred, her green eyes gone again. Maggots poured from the empty sockets tumbling end over end down her pale face.

"I am here for you. I'm going to take you away from here," she said. "It'll all be over soon."

This was the most unforgiving he had ever seen her. This was it then, her moment of retribution. But he didn't want to die. He never meant for her to die either. He didn't mean for anyone to die. It was just so unfair.

Roger looked from Alice to the open doorway, and he didn't think he would be able to make it. He didn't know what she planned to do once she got a hold of him, but he knew it wasn't going to be good. It was like her father's fury had suddenly gotten into her. Her eyes blazed with a fire, literally. There were flames spitting from her cavernous eye sockets, sending fire into the air before her as she roared her anger.

Alice walked with purpose. Her anger would only be staunched by feeding her thirst for vengeance. He wasn't as ready to give in to that demand as he had thought he was when he came home to face her. He didn't want this.

"Please don't kill me. Please. I don't want to die."

Alice's hands were reaching toward him. "What are you so afraid of? What do you see, Roger? Is Dad here too?"

Roger screamed and bounded over the back of the couch.

Roger saw Alice closing in on him. He realized then that her feet didn't touch the ground. They hovered above it, toes pointed down. She floated toward him even as she looked like she was marching into war, the flames from her empty eyes licking at the air, maggots crawling through it and burning themselves alive to topple to the carpet.

He quickly scrambled to his feet and escaped her deadly touch. Her fingertips narrowly missed his shoulder. "I need you to come with me now."

Roger's heart felt like it was going to explode. It was boxing with his chest cavity.

Where was her father? He had to be here somewhere too. She mentioned him herself. It was his anger that had fueled her, turned her into this. She did seem bigger somehow, adult sized, despite looking the same age she always was and would always be, thanks to him.

Maybe Alice's anger, her hatred, her need for retribution, had fed her spirit until it grew and became more powerful. Maybe that was what she needed to finally destroy him. Maybe all of this was just to buy time until she was powerful enough to see this through.

Maybe her father was stepping back to allow her to have this moment because it belonged to her. Maybe he was proudly watching from the sideline somewhere, encouraging her to do it, to vanquish their enemy.

But I'm not ready! I don't want to die!

Roger knew one thing for sure. He wanted to live. He needed to live, to survive, to escape somehow and awaken to see tomorrow. With this in mind, Roger ran past the floating Alice and headed for the kitchen.

"Why are you running from me?" she shouted behind him. "Don't fight me, Roger."

He surged with adrenaline. He was propelled by survival, driven. Roger looked over his shoulder and saw Alice rise higher into the air behind him. She turned 180 degrees without moving a muscle, then she started for him again, anger blazing in her fiery eyes, her pale face dead set on killing him, a scream on her lips.

Roger tore open a drawer and retrieved the biggest knife he owned. Then he turned at last to find Alice right there, screaming face and flaming eyes about to come down upon him.

"Don't fight. It's okay," she told him. "It's all going to be okay now, Rodge."

Then her mouth opened further and further, unnaturally, as if it were being cranked. It looked as if she were about to swallow him whole.

Roger released a silent scream of his own as Alice descended upon him, hands outstretched, pale fingers curled like claws, with long, black, razor-sharp talons replacing her fingernails, except for the one missing nail. Roger didn't even know if it was possible to stab a ghost, but he was damned well going to try.

As she grabbed hold of him, he lashed out with the knife. It went in but she still grabbed at him, her icy fingers clutching his shoulders. He pushed harder and harder, not knowing if it was even doing any good.

She continued to grasp at him until she took him down to the floor. He screamed and rolled. She lunged at him, claws out, and her impossibly stretched mouth opened wide enough to swallow him, razor teeth gnashing like she was actually going to eat him, to consume him whole right there on his living room floor. She coughed and choked like she did the day she died. He could hear it like it was coming from everywhere.

Roger screamed and plunged the knife into her chest, and she finally froze. He lowered her to the ground, her mouth frozen in its wide-open posture. He had killed her once before, by accident, and now he had to kill her again on purpose. Roger cried and apologized as he pulled the knife free and then plunged it back into her. He did it over and over. And over still.

"I didn't want this. I didn't want any of this," he cried. "I wanted you to forgive me, to set me free."

Roger could feel someone watching from the open doorway. Maybe it was her father or his own. He turned to face the doorway, and something hit him, knocking him off his feet.

"No!" he screamed. "I won't let you kill me! This is your fault. If you weren't so violent, I wouldn't have needed to protect her! It's because of you and your damned anger that this all happened! You hear me? It's because of you!"

Alice's father didn't respond. His own father did. "I didn't do this. You did. This was you,, you hear me? No one else. You."

Roger was pinned to the ground by an incredible force. His arms were restrained behind him, and he couldn't break free. He screamed and screamed and screamed some more, thrashing as he did. "Let go of me! You were evil before you died. You're the reason I was always so scared, my whole life!"

"Who do you think I am?" his father said to him as he held Roger to the ground under his full body weight. He used something to painfully secure Roger's wrists. "You just killed this woman. No one else did that. You did." Then he spoke to somebody else. "I need back up. This guy is hallucinating. I think he's on something. There's a deceased female. Neighbor across the hall said the woman was trying to help him but the guy just lost it. He won't stop fighting. Guy thinks I'm his father or something. It's bad in here."

33

MARK STEPHENSON LOOKED at Roger through a window. "How's he doing?" he asked a man in a business suit who stood nearby.

"Not much change yet, but it will take time for the medication to get into his system and really start working."

Mark nodded. "Does he... understand?"

"Somewhat. He understands he killed his sister, but he believes he was tricked into it by the ghost that was haunting him. He did also admit he stopped taking his medication days before the violence. I believe it very much had an effect on the outcome."

Mark nodded. "Alright. Well, I can see that he's in good hands. I just wanted to come by and check on him. I feel like I failed him. I discovered he hadn't filled his prescription, and I tried to get a hold of him, but I was never able to. I called and left messages, but I should have tried harder. I should have gone by his place. I should have known something was wrong the last time I spoke to him. I should have pursued it. I didn't think he would do this. He seemed so far from violence. I just missed it."

The other doctor nodded. "I understand how you feel, Mark, but you can't put this on yourself. I would probably feel the same way, but rest assured it isn't you. Roger is very ill. It's obvious you care for him and all your patients. You can only do what you can do. You can't save them all. Besides, if you had gone by his place, you may have ended up like his sister."

Mark frowned. "I guess you're right. It's not always an easy thing to accept though, at least not without Jim Beam." He laughed and the other doctor laughed with him. "Please let me know if there is any change, Peter."

"Absolutely. I will let you know immediately. The guy doesn't have anyone else really. His mother is alive, but she doesn't live around here, and we haven't been able to get ahold of her as of yet. His sister was all he had."

Mark exhaled his defeat. "Alright. I'll work on getting a hold of the mother. That's something I might be able to help with." He shook the doctor's hand and then made his way out of the mental ward.

Inside the room, Roger sat on the ground, back to the wall and knees to his chest, rocking back and forth. Alice stood before him and watched, her eyes full of sadness. He matched her gaze when he looked back at her.

"I'm glad you're back on your medication and you're clear," she said to him. "Now you can see me and hear me."

"I don't want to," Roger said, shaking his head.

"But I tried to help you for so long," the young girl said, tears falling from her emerald eyes. "You wanted me to forgive you. I forgave you right away, Roger. It was you who wouldn't forgive yourself. You kept seeing your own version of me. I don't know what you saw, but it seemed so frightening, and I kept trying to tell you it wasn't me, but I could never get through. I'm so sorry."

Roger stared at her for a moment. The truth hit him then as

his eyes fell on her, looking how she did before death, innocent and sweet, her face pale and unmarred. He trembled, tears filling his eyes. "The two Alices," he said then. "The dark Alice wasn't real."

Alice shook her head. Her bottom lip turned up and quivered. "I'm sorry. I tried to tell you. I wrote things because your head wouldn't always let you see me without your meds. Your neighbors saw me. They tried to tell you too. I gave you my doll because it always made me feel better. Old lady Agatha, she can speak to all of us. I told her what was happening. She told you I was sad. No one could reach you. I'm so sorry, Roger. I never wanted you to hurt like this."

"Writing? The elevator doors...the laundry powder. My neighbors. Rebecca talking about my daughter. Jesus. Agatha told me you wanted me to stop. I didn't know what I was doing. Oh my God. It was all me. I killed Kara. It was all me."

He started to shake, racked with sobs.

Kara appeared behind Alice. She put a hand on the child's shoulder. "It will take him time," Kara told her. "But we need to go back. Your father misses you and the building is waiting for us."

"Kara," Roger said, crawling forward and reaching up toward her. "Oh my God, Kara!" But his sister and Alice both dissipated as if they were made of gas, dispersing into the air. Just like that, Roger was alone again, and he screamed in pain, falling onto his side, and curling up into the fetal position, where he continued his sobbing.

34

MARK WALKED through the halls of the Twin Spirits mental hospital until he reached the exit. They took good care of people here, and it was obvious that doctors like Peter Mansfield cared about their patients, but something about the place made him uncomfortable. He needed to get out in a hurry anyway. He had another appointment that would be at his office any minute.

Mark drove quickly, all too eager to leave the hospital grounds, and to leave his failure with Roger behind and move on to someone he could actually help. When he got back to the office, he saw there was a car other than Jessica's parked outside.

"Dammit," he said, realizing his patient had gotten there before him. He quickly threw the car into park and hurried inside.

Jessica smiled from behind her desk. "I let her in. She hasn't been here too long. I brought scones from the bakery on the corner. I gave her yours, and a glass of water to wash it down."

"You're a lifesaver," Mark told her. Then he hurried past her into his office.

There was an attractive young Asian woman sitting in one of the chairs before his desk who turned and waved shyly when he entered. Mark gave her a big wide smile and a wave of his own. "Hey there. Sorry, you beat me here, Sarah, was it? I'm Dr. Stephenson, but you can call me Mark. I don't like formal titles.

I want you to think of me as a friend, and to promote that, I will forgive you for eating my scone."

The woman's eyes went wide. "I'm sorry. I didn't know it was yours."

Mark laughed as he took his seat behind his desk. "Relax. I'm kidding. I don't even like scones. I just don't have the heart to tell Jessica that."

Sarah laughed and Mark felt like he had successfully broken the ice.

"So, what brings you to see me, Sarah?"

Sarah's smile fell away. "This is gonna sound crazy," she said.

Mark smiled reassuringly. "You'd be surprised what I hear every day. Try me."

Sarah nodded. She took a big deep breath and exhaled slowly to steady her nerves. "Okay," she said, placing her palms flat on her thighs, and smoothing her dress. "Well, I don't know if you've heard of it, but I live at the Sunnycrest Apartments on the other side of the city, and I think it's haunted. I think there's a ghost that wants something from me now, and I don't know what to do. Isn't that nuts?"

"Not at all," Mark said with a smile that didn't at all match what he felt inside. "I don't think that sounds even a little crazy. You'll find I'm pretty open minded, Sarah. I'm glad you came to see me."

Deep down, Mark was terrified. He was terrified Sarah would be another failure, another like Maria and Roger that would just end up in Twin Pines. How did they all find their way to him? There were many psychiatrists in a city this size. It was starting to seem like there was something that tied him to Sunnycrest just like Roger and the others, something that wouldn't let him go. He felt trapped, haunted in his own right, and he gently tugged at his collar, pulling it away from his neck.

After a deep breath of his own, Mark gave his best smile and said, "Sarah, why don't you start from the beginning and tell me what happened."

ACKNOWLEDGMENTS

There are many people to thank in these back pages. First and foremost, thanks to you, the reader, for giving me a reason to write and making it worthwhile. Contact me and I will put your true names in this section of the next book, for real...I mean it.

I need to thank Robin and the girls for being my muses and critics and supporting this wild adventure, and Robin's mother for her emotional and financial support as well. Ella Skeen, thank you for your fantastic ideas that always seem to get published and Julia for being a wonderful writer who has been published along side me. I will be forever proud of that moment. Thank you to Boe Benjiro for teaching me how to be productive and write novels during the small span of a baby's nap, and just for being the coolest kid that has ever lived.

I need to thank my brother, Christopher Healy, for showing me at a young age that there is more out there than children's books. It was a defining moment in my life when he turned me on to horror and helped me find my destiny. And thanks in the same regard to my brother from another mother, Jesse Knight for joining me on my earliest creative endeavors.

I need to thank my mother, Margaret Healy, and my father, Bill Healy, for always encouraging reading and writing and not listening to a terrified administration that urged them to steer me away from horror.

Thank you to Christina Spetz, because without you this book would never have happened. Most readers don't know but this series and first book were a long time in the making. Over a decade ago, it was Christina who helped me come up with the concept and fine tune it. You are an incredible muse and I hope you read this finished product and feel satisfied with it.

I need to thank Gary Smith and James Holt who have supported me for what feels like forever, buying all my little self published books before I was anyone with anything real to offer. You guys are the best.

Thank you to Nic Campbell, and his mother Erin Campbell who have been not just creative supporters but family for the last umpteen thousand years or so, even if we've drifted apart in recent days. I will always love and appreciate you.

On that note, I must thank Soda Clements and Mama Gloria (a name now more fitting than it once was) and her sister T.T. who are my freak clan for life. From childhood to the end of the rainbow. I could not have ever accomplished anything without that troop.

Thanks to Ron Bargine for his support, amazing artwork and lifelong friendship. Thanks to Bardi and his clan as well.

Thanks endlessly to Kelly Lynn Colby, the most amazing editor in the world who pushed me to be my best even when it made me want to bang my head into the wall. Thank you so much for believing in this book and series and working so hard to help me make it what it is. Thanks also to Tracy and the rest of Cursed Dragon Ship, my happy home. Thanks as well to Cover Villain for their hard work in making this presentable. Also thanks to the Asheville coffee shops, the Grind and Izzy's, where I wrote a lot of this book.

Thanks to all the small press publishers that believed in me and encouraged me and befriended me on my way to this point. I have shared the pages of so many wonderful anthologies with some truly fantastic people. In no particular order: David Green, Natalie Brown, Brandi and Shelly and the BIF crew, the Macabre Ladies and all the wonderful writers I met and hung out on zoom with during the pandemic due to them. Michelle River and the Eerie River crew for teaching me some very humbling and valuable lessons and remaining my friend while I learned them. Richard and Dee and the Fox Hollow gang. David Paul for his incredible art and incredible heart. Scott and the folks at Queer Sci-fi. Dawn and her crew. Mark Young, Josh Taylor, Tim Mendees, Ruth Ann, and so many more. If I didn't mention your name, I didn't forget you. You're probably in the aforementioned crews and I love you dearly and will do my best to support all your creative endeavors.

Thank you to KC, Michelle, Lisa, Heather and all my amazing cousins of who their are too many to name, but I love you all. Thanks to my Aunt Kate for always being moral support and inspiration and my Aunt Jo for the same. Thanks endlessly to my Uncle Jim for inspiring everything I am. I would not be half the wordsmith had it not been for your smartass wit and teachings. I love you always and I hope you are smiling down from heaven to see me finally succeed.

Last, but certainly not least, thank you to Simon Clark, my favorite author, hero, and inspiration, for being everything a hero should be. I hope one day I can be for a budding writer what you have been for me. Thank you so much!

ABOUT THE AUTHOR

Chisto Healy has been writing since his brother handed him Dean Koontz's *Servants of Twilight* at age nine. His hero and favorite author is Simon Clark, so go read him right now. Chisto's got a lot of great stuff of his own coming out and you can find all the details at https://chistohealy.blogspot.com which he does his best to keep updated. There are almost 20 books coming out with his work in them. He lives in North Carolina with his beautiful and wacky fiancée, her chill mom, three of the most creative and awesome kids the world has to offer, and a plethora of kickass pets. Please reach out. He would love to hear from you. You can also follow him on Amazon.

If you see petals gray as thunder, leaves red as the setting sun, you run. Always run.

9 781951 445218